# ANXIETY
## THE AGORA VIRUS BOOK 2

## JACK HUNT

DIRECT RESPONSE PUBLISHING

ISBN-13: 978-1542808217
ISBN-10: 1542808219

# Dedication

For my family.

# Prologue

Frank Talbot felt a bead of sweat trickle down his back as he yanked the blade free from the second tire. It hissed hard as it deflated. Fear shot through him along with a great deal of satisfaction. Fair? I will give you fair, he thought.

A hard noonday sun beat down, and heat waves danced across the parking lot that contained only a few vehicles. The place had become a ghost town. He'd spent the better part of fifteen minutes tracking him down and now he was only seconds away from getting even.

He shuffled over to the black-and-white vehicle, pressed his back against the door and remained in a crouched position. He took the small red gasoline canister in hand and slid over to the rear door. Rising up just a little to make sure that the coast was still clear, he eyed the men inside the café.

They had no idea.

He pulled open the door and slipped inside, unscrewed the top, and began to douse the front seats, the floor, and then the rear. When the vehicle was thoroughly soaked, he backed out making sure to stay low.

Out of sight. Out of mind.

Leaving the door open he continued backing up, leaving a thick trail of gasoline along the ground as he made his way back into the nearby tree line. The stench of gas lingered in the air, teasing him to light it.

He panted, his chest rose and fell and still a smile danced on his lips.

Once inside the covering of dense trees, he glanced at his watch. His eyes darted to the young kid sitting on a bench across the street. In a matter of minutes, the kid would walk into the café and hand the note to him.

Oh, he wanted to stick around to see his face when he lit it, but Sal had been adamant. They needed to be long gone by the time he came out. He was right, of course. Sal was right about many things and he usually listened to him — except for this one time.

When they had stopped on the outskirts of Lowville on the long journey home, Frank had told the others that he needed to pick up some gas and a few supplies but that wasn't the truth. Sal knew it.

He'd been giving him the evil eye ever since Frank mentioned it.

Frank stared at his watch, his mind drifted back to that conversation.

*"Are you out of your mind?" Sal asked.*

*"I've never been clearer."*

*"We could get tossed in jail."*

*"Look around you, Sal, do you really think society is going back to the way it was?"*

*Sal stared at him as he filled the canister with gas. The others lingered around the SUV, chatting among themselves blissfully unaware of what he was about to do. It was criminal but so was what had been done to them.*

*"You know, Frank, I get it. Really, I do, but you know he won't let it go."*

*The gasoline reached the top of the canister and Frank screwed the top back on. A large sign positioned out front of the gas station said, GET GAS WHILE YOU CAN. CLOSING SOON.*

*"Listen, just fill up the SUV, and the other canister and I will be back soon."*

*"And if it goes wrong?"*

*"It won't."*

*Sal shook his head in frustration. He ran a hand across his bearded jaw. Both of them were beginning to look like they had spent far too long in the outback. It had been over nine hours since they had left Queens. What should have taken them seven hours to get back to Clayton, New York, was taking far longer because the roads were clogged up with folks trying to escape the city. Now they were only an hour away from the safety of home. The roads were clearer the farther north they went but they still felt like salmon trying to swim upstream.*

"If I'm not back in thirty minutes, you get the hell out of here."

Sal let out a heavy sigh. "And what if he's not there?"

"Then we leave. Okay? No harm done."

"You aren't coming back in thirty minutes, are you?"

Frank turned back to Sal. His mind was lost in what he was going to do.

"Keep the engine running. You have my word."

One way or another that asshole was going to pay. It hadn't left his mind since leaving Lowville the first time around. And now the situation in the country had become even worse, he knew that the boundary line between what was right and wrong had been blurred. Total anarchy had erupted across the United States as barricades had been breached and the Agora virus had spread rapidly.

He turned to leave and Ella spotted him. "Dad?"

"Just stay in the vehicle, I'll be back soon."

He didn't stick around to get into a discussion with her. If anyone might have been able to change his mind, it was his daughter. She had a way of talking him down from the edge.

*She had been the first one to see him try to take his life. Back when his illness had taken him to his lowest point. She had walked in on him with a gun in his mouth.*

Frank shook his head, focusing back on the task at hand. He watched the young kid mutter something to his friend and they grabbed up their bikes and cycled across the street to the café. Frank held the Zippo lighter, struck it and a blue flame flickered to life against a faint wind. He tossed it down and watched it ignite the trail of gasoline. Like a heat-seeking missile finding its way to a target, the blue and orange flame spread. He turned and began to run, anticipating a massive explosion.

*Five seconds. Ten seconds. Twenty seconds.*

*Still nothing?*

He twisted and squinted through the trees. He could barely see the parking lot now. *C'mon!*

His head swept from side to side. He remembered what Sal had said. He glanced at his watch again. Eight minutes remained.

*Just leave. Go, get away from here.*

Now, perhaps it was his OCD kicking in, that incessant need to make sure everything was done just right, but he couldn't let it go. He had to see what had gone wrong.

He dashed back towards the parking lot.

Once he retraced his steps to the tree line he saw what had happened. He hadn't used enough gas inside the vehicle and without it trickling down onto the ground, there was no connection. The trail had fallen short by half a foot at least from the vehicle.

*Shit!*

The flame was nearly out. He spotted the silver Zippo on the ground; he darted out into the clearing, scooped it up, and raced towards the cruiser. And tossed the open flame into the vehicle.

\* \* \*

Minutes earlier, inside the café, there were very few people seated. Chester was squeezed into a corner, minding his own business with a newspaper in hand, reading the update on the outbreak.

"All scare tactics. What do you think, Bud?" Chester asked Bud Traymore, the owner of the Shed, a small café that had catered to the locals for as long as Chester had lived in Lowville.

"I think it's starting to hurt my bottom line. The past two days have been terrible. Besides you, I've only had nine other customers. Everyone is staying away from here. It's those damn headlines. '*Avoid Crowds.*' Like, are they trying to kill my business?"

Chester chuckled. He glanced up at the shrill of a bell above the door. Two young teenagers froze in place.

"There you go, Bud, things are looking up," he said.

Bud snorted and kept wiping down the counter. Chester went back to eating his pie and reading the article when he noticed out of his peripheral vision the kids staring at him.

"Well if you are going to stand there and gawk, at least tell me why?"

He put his fork down and the tallest of the two, with a buzz cut, rushed over and dropped a piece of paper in

14

front of him. Chester looked the kid up and down. He couldn't have been more than thirteen, with ginger hair and more freckles than anyone should have had.

"He told us to give you this," the boy blurted out.

Chester's brow knit together. "Who?"

He shrugged and looked outside towards an empty seat across the street. "Some guy."

Chester looked confused as he stared down at the torn piece of paper. He was about to turn it over to read what it said, when an explosion of epic proportions erupted outside. Startled, he nearly fell off his chair. He jumped up from his seat, screeching it back, and tossed down the napkin in his hand.

"What the fuck?"

His cruiser had gone up in flames. His eyes darted from side to side and then he spotted him — at least the back of him — as he sprinted into a cluster of overgrown oak trees. Chester scowled, snatched up his wallet and keys, and rushed outside. He lifted an arm to shield his eyes as the flames crept higher.

The paper was still in his hand. He turned it over to see what it said.

Scribbled in blue ink was the following: *Here's that gasoline I owe you.*

He balled his fists, and immediately got on the radio as he took off in pursuit of the man he thought he would never see again.

*Bastard!*

"Davis, where are you?"

"Over on the west side dealing with a domestic. Lady is sick, and someone…"

"Where's Martell?"

"He called in sick."

"Anyone else?"

He panted hard as he pushed his way through the trees, and thick brush. In the distance he could see that bastard getting away. He had a good mind to pull his piece and fire off a round but that would only mean a shitload of paperwork and besides, this was going to raise too many questions. He could hear it now. *Why did he set your cruiser on fire? What's this about you and your cousins destroying his vehicle and beating them up?*

Davis came back over the radio. It crackled. "Sorry, boss, we are short-staffed with all this sickness."

"Fuck," Chester yelled as he nearly fell ass over tit trying to catch up. He wasn't getting any younger and this asshole already had a head start on him.

When he eventually broke out of the tree line on the other side of the patch of woodland, it was too late. An SUV tore away. Chester placed a hand against a tree. He was huffing and panting hard. He wiped his brow with the back of his hand.

"I know where you live!" he shouted. His voice was lost in the sound of the wind. He smashed his fist at the air as if trying to knock out an opponent. "Son of a bitch!"

## Chapter 1

Dry blood pooled around his head. Frank stared at the body of Bob Riley. Fifty-nine years of age, married and with a family of six, he had operated Clayton Marina Sales and Services for as long as Frank had lived in the area. After making it safely back to Clayton, they were faced with their first challenge. There were no boats. The one they had left behind was gone from the dock, and Gloria wasn't answering her phone.

The situation in the small town had become dire and they were only witnessing the tip of the iceberg. Usually the showroom was full of NauticStar, G3, and Skeeter boats and all manner of new and used vessels but now it was stripped bare. Everything was gone from the lot and the showroom. Glass crunched beneath his boots as he backed up from the grisly sight.

Had he been trying to help someone? The gaping wound on the back of his head left no doubt as to how he had died. Someone had taken what they wanted by force. Frank shook his head, unable to comprehend that someone would have done this to a man that would have given the shirt off his back.

"Frank, we should go," Sal said as he tugged at his arm and broke him out of his trance-like state. Frank turned and Sal walked back outside through the shattered showroom window. He tried again to phone Gloria but got no response. Where are the police? The parking lot of the marina was jam-packed with abandoned vehicles. They assumed people had tried escaping to one of the islands in the St. Lawrence River, or had headed into Canada. By the reports on the radio, Canada wasn't doing any better. The Agora virus was out of control and making its way from large cities into smaller towns.

Upon entering Clayton, they had immediately noticed how barren the streets were. It was like a ghost town. With no boat to get them across to the island, they had decided to see what still remained. All they saw was the aftermath of looting and rioting. There were burned-out establishments and the road was littered with garbage, glass, and metal shutters that had been torn from the front of stores.

Driving slowly through the streets, weaving around vehicles and all manner of discarded carts from the grocery store, they decided to see if the police department was still operating. Though Frank wasn't keen to head over there, Sal knew a number of them as clients and wanted to see what was being done to maintain order.

"Seems pretty clear to me. Nothing!" Frank muttered.

Frank wasn't the only one that was skittish about running to the law. Zach was still reeling from having killed a soldier. Even though they didn't expect anyone to come looking for him, it didn't alleviate their anxiety.

Fortunately, one glance at the police station answered the question about whether or not they were still on duty. The doors had been smashed in. The American flag at the side of the building had been burned, and it looked as though the right section of the property had been torched.

Frank's eyes widened. Someone had literally driven a minivan through the front windows. The whole thing was scorched black, nothing but a charred shell.

"Wait here," Frank said to the others as he and Sal went in to explore and assess the situation. At the bare minimum, perhaps they could find a weapon. The very mention of it made Gabriel chuckle.

"You're wasting your time. Do you really think whoever drove that vehicle through the front window did it just to show their hate for the cops?"

"Just sit tight."

Frank climbed the three stone steps that led up to the destroyed door on the left, while Sal went to the right. They waited at the entrance for a few seconds. Frank glanced over his shoulder at Ella who was standing beside the SUV looking around.

Both of them crept inside, glass crunched beneath their boots.

"Wyatt Barnes?" Sal called out, hoping to find the officer they had met before leaving Clayton. There was no answer. In fact, there was no sound. It was eerily quiet. Scattered all over the corridor were folders and papers, lots of paperwork. A gust of wind blew in and some of it lifted in the air. The smell of death reached Frank's nostrils. It was an odor he was beginning to get used to. The highway had been littered with those who had succumbed to the virus. Wild animals had begun to chew away at the flesh of the unfortunate, while others sat slumped over in their vehicles.

Covered with face masks, and disposable overalls, Sal ducked into the main office and Frank followed. The smell of death was strong. Tables had been overturned. It was a mess, and yet there were no dead bodies at least that they could see. But there had to be as the place reeked.

"Split up, I'll check the back rooms, you search the front offices. Check the desks, cupboards, see if you can find an armor room."

"Do you want me to check the basement?" a voice said behind them. Frank spun on his heels to find Tyrell gazing around.

"Didn't I tell you to wait outside?"

"You also wanted me to stay in Watertown," he replied before walking off and ignoring Frank. The first stop along the way had been to take Tyrell to his home in Watertown. As hard as the journey was with strangers tucked into the back of the SUV, filling it out like a sardine can, he had hoped that Watertown would have been in better shape than it was. It wasn't. Tyrell found his parents dead, eliminating any chance of leaving him there. Now Frank had more people to think about. He cursed under his breath. It wasn't just dealing with a lethal virus that bothered him; it was all the mouths he was going to have to feed. He had stocked up well before leaving but that was only enough for Sal's family, Ella, and him. It was meant to last at least six months, now with four more, they would be lucky if it lasted a month.

Frank was still glaring towards the spot where Tyrell had been when Sal tapped him on the arm. "Get used to it, Frank."

"That's the thing. I don't want to."

They made their way through the deserted station, checking different offices, lockers, and cupboards but there was nothing. Whoever had attacked the station had made a point to strip it of anything that was of benefit. No ammo. No guns. Hell, there wasn't even any tea or coffee.

Then he heard Tyrell's voice.

"Yo! Mr. T."

"God, I wish he would stop calling me that," Frank said.

"I dunno, it kind of fits. Mr. T was a grumpy bastard as well."

They wandered back through the main office, out into the corridor and down a flight of steps into the basement. "Where are you?"

"Change room."

As soon as he pushed his way inside the change room, it became clear where the smell of death was coming from. Frank instinctively backed up. Everything being close to the infected, alive or dead, still made his skin crawl.

Slumped down on the floor next to a locker was a cop. Frank couldn't tell who he was but he had obviously been dead a while, as his skin had changed in color. During his time in Iraq he had seen how quickly a body decomposed and the different stages of death from rigor mortis setting in, hands and feet changing color, to blood pooling in lower parts of the body. The skin would then become purplish and waxy as rigor mortis exited, and the head and neck would turn a greenish-blue color. That usually kicked in at the twenty-four-hour mark. Around that time was when the strong smell of rotting meat could turn a person's stomach.

Three days later, the body gases created blisters on the skin, fluids leaked from the mouth, nose, eyes, ears and rectum, and then week's later skin, hair, and nails became so loose they could be pulled from the body.

It was a sick sight but not half as bad as what he was seeing now. The effects of the Agora virus were brutal. People suffered horrifically, and death was painful.

Tyrell went to reach for the sidearm that was still in the holster when Frank yelled at him. "Wait!"

He paused, and Sal shot him a glance. "We need it, Frank."

"I know we do," he said swallowing hard and reaching into his pocket to pull out sanitizers. Tyrell was wearing gloves and a mask, which had been one of the requirements of having them in the vehicle with them. Still, the sick had touched that Glock 22, which meant it was now smothered in deadly germs. What if they couldn't get them all off? They would have to strip it down and sterilize it fully. This wasn't just about giving it a simple cleaning with solvent. He would need to do it. How else could he know if they had done it correctly? One cleaning wouldn't be enough. He squeezed his eyes shut at the very thought of getting close to it.

"Breathe, Frank."

He nodded. "Go ahead, take it."

They were home, but safe? That was still to be determined. At least now they had a weapon.

# Chapter 2

There was no way that any of them were going to be able to swim to the island. It was too far. The current was strong and besides, without a boat they weren't going to be able to gather what they needed over the coming months. Sal made the suggestion to check Fishers Landing or Collins Landing or one of the many homes along the waterfront. Worst-case scenario they would have to cross the bridge over to Wellesley Island State Park and swim the short distance to Grindstone and then ask the Guthrie brothers for assistance.

That was the last thing Frank wanted to do.

It was getting late; darkness would soon make it even more difficult to find what they wanted. All of them were hungry from having not eaten in close to twenty-four hours.

"How about we stay at our place tonight? We can find a boat tomorrow," Ella said. "I'm exhausted, I know the rest of them are."

Frank glanced over to the others who were leaning against the SUV as if they had hiked up Mount Everest. *Youngsters*, he thought, shaking his head.

"What do you think, Sal?"

Sal had been beside himself with worry ever since Queens. The last time he'd spoken to his wife was when they were on their way down to collect Ella but since then she hadn't answered the phone. It wasn't like her. Frank agreed and though he was more than willing to spend the evening searching for a boat, he thought it was best that the others rested and ate. His apartment in Clayton wasn't big, so they opted to head over to Sal's place, which was a blue clapboard house at the end of Franklin Street. It backed up against the local recreational park called Lions Field. The location had originally been a dump owned by the State of New York but it ended up being maintained as a public field for the Lions Club and Clayton Village.

"Yeah, maybe Gloria headed back to the house," Sal

replied.

"Okay, well let's at least get these guys some food and you and I can head out later."

He nodded but didn't say any more. His features hardened and it was clear his worry was getting worse.

They made their way over to the house and each of them breathed a sigh of relief as they got inside. It was warm but humid because the windows and doors hadn't been opened. The smell of food that had gone off lingered in the air.

"Gloria? Adrian? Bailey?" Sal shot up the stairs and checked the rooms but no one was in the house. It also appeared as if no one had broken in, as everything was exactly the way he'd left it. Sal went over to his neighbor's house to see if he was around but returned a few minutes later, shrugging.

"It's just like a whole bunch of folks upped and left."

Gabriel slumped down in a chair on the opposite side of where Hayley was. "They can't have all left. People don't just run off when a virus hits."

Ella jabbed him. "No?"

"C'mon, I didn't have much choice."

"Maybe it's the same with others," Tyrell said flicking on the TV. All it came back with was white noise. None of the stations were working. The media had abandoned their posts. It was to be expected. The upswing was the electricity was still working. It was small things that meant a lot now. How long the power grid would remain up was anyone's guess.

"So what have you got to eat?" Hayley asked.

Sal looked too distracted to answer so Frank went into the kitchen and began rooting around in the cupboards. He emerged with several cans of beans, Spam, and soup.

"It's not great, but it will do for now. Ella, you want to give me a hand?"

"I'll help," Hayley said rising to her feet, entering the kitchen and snatching a can out of Frank's hand. His eyebrows shot up and Ella shook her head before joining her.

"So you got any movies?" Tyrell asked while fishing

around near the TV.

"No," Sal replied. "And get away from there."

Tyrell's hands shot up. "Okay, easy, brother. Just asking."

Over the course of the next fifteen minutes, Frank went through the process of sanitizing the handgun using household items such as boiling water, white vinegar and a bottle of hydrogen peroxide. He followed up with WD-40 and lubricated all the parts using a few drops of motor oil.

"Listen, guys, we're going to shoot out and see if we can't find a boat. Eat, rest, we'll be back later."

Ella poked her head out from the kitchen. "You want me to come?"

"No, it's fine. Probably best you stay here and keep an eye on..." he trailed off gesturing his head to Tyrell who was ignoring Sal's request and fishing through a collection of DVDs.

"Oh, we just hit the mother lode!" Zach hollered while holding up a bottle of bourbon, which he'd found inside one of the cupboards in the living room.

"That's not yours."

"Sal. Let's go," Frank said trying to get him to leave before things got out of hand. He was on edge, and rightfully so. Frank would have been climbing the walls by now if Ella and Kate had been by themselves on the island.

As they walked outside, Frank tried to get through to Kate again but he got no answer. It had been the same way since Queens. However, unlike Sal, he at least knew that Kate was safe behind the walls of the CDC building. At least he thought she was. Reality was, they were all clinging to a shard of hope that could easily be shattered with one phone call or an update on the radio.

"I don't like leaving them here."

"They'll be fine. Let's go," Frank said, giving one last glance towards the house.

Over the following half an hour they went up and down the waterfront, stopping at various homes that had docks. They figured someone would have a kayak, or a canoe. It was common in the summer to see the river filled with fishermen, and families out in rowboats, pedal boats, and kayaks. The problem was, in the time they had been away, the outbreak had forced people to rethink how they could survive. A large majority of people might have attempted to head over to Canada, or one of the Thousand Islands. Many of the islands had more than one property on them. The smallest, like Frank's, had one while Grindstone Island had ten year-round households. The population then swelled to seven hundred in the summer months when visitors toured the island.

The SUV bumped up and down as they drove up a dirt driveway towards a large cottage. By now it was pitch-dark outside. As the headlights lit up the front of the house, Frank saw an inside light turn on then off.

"Did you see that?" he muttered.

"Yeah, maybe we should skip this one."

"Sal, if we don't find one, one of us is going to have to swim across."

"Well it isn't going to be me, and it certainly won't be

you. I say we get that Zach kid to do it. He looks like a strong lad."

Frank chuckled as he killed the engine and hopped out. Like many of the homes along the waterfront, this one had a large yard that surrounded the house. The property was just off Jackson Lane. It wasn't that everyone would have abandoned their homes, but based on what they had seen so far, residents must have had the same idea of grabbing a boat and getting the fuck out of dodge. At night, it was hard to see if there were any boats. Usually there would have been lots. Most properties along the waterfront would have one or two.

As they made their way around the house and down to the dock, Frank kind of wished they had kept the gun on them. They had left it with the others just in case they encountered any issues. They just assumed that if anyone was still in Clayton they were locked up inside their homes. Windows had been boarded up on many houses to prevent people from getting in. People were smart. They might not have all been proactive in preparing for the worst scenario, but they certainly were taking measures since.

"Why aren't you talking about them?"

"Who?" Frank asked.

"You know."

He was referring to the Guthries. The thought of them revisiting his island had crossed his mind several times after leaving but he didn't discuss it, as he didn't want to stress Sal out any more than he was.

Frank glanced at him as they continued down a steep incline heading for a dock.

"We don't know if they visited, Sal."

"Oh, I know. There is no way in hell she wouldn't answer."

"Look, let's just get a boat and…"

Sal grabbed a hold of him by the scruff of the neck. "If anything has happened to them I swear…"

Frank's face twisted up. "You swear what? Remember, you were the one that chose to come with me. I tried to persuade you to stay."

There was an awkward moment. He held tight for a few seconds more.

Sal slowly released his grip knowing Frank was right. The fact was he could have stayed but for one reason or another he had chosen to go to Queens. Frank knew that it may have cost him but the way he saw it, that's what they were dealing with now — a whole bunch of unknowns.

A step left, a step right, a word spoken out of line and any one of them could find their head on the chopping board. It wasn't just a virus that was a threat; it was the ruthless and desperate, neighbors, and old friends. People would go to great lengths to survive. How far was still to be determined but the future certainly looked dangerous.

Frank continued on his way until he reached the dock.

"Bingo!" He pointed to a small boat that was covered in a tarp and branches. Loose leaves had been scattered over and around the area in an attempt to cover it up. Sal shone the light in front of them as Frank moved forward to grab a branch off.

"Frank!" Sal suddenly hollered, grabbing him back just as the sound of a wire snapping dispersed air in front of them. Both of them collapsed on the dock, and felt it shift beneath. Once Frank had managed to catch his breath, he started berating Sal.

"What the hell are you playing at?"

Sal pointed his flashlight ahead. A thin metal wire was strung between two trees. Whether it was a booby trap or some kind of an alarm system was hard to tell but it sure as hell would have torn into them. Frank got up and shuffled over to the wire and touched it like a guitar string.

"Someone didn't want anyone getting their hands on that boat. C'mon, help me get the tarp off."

"No, we need to get out of here. Find another one," Sal said turning to leave.

"After what we just went through. Screw that," Frank replied, kneeling on the edge of the dock and tugging at the tarp rope. He hadn't untied more than two of the knots when the sound of a shotgun being cocked behind them made them freeze.

## Chapter 3

"That's it," the stranger's voice bellowed. "Back up."

"Look, we—" Frank barely managed to turn his head before the stranger fired a round near his feet to make damn sure they knew he meant business. A chunk of wood hit his leg, leaving a gaping hole in the dock.

They threw up their hands. "Whoa!"

"I don't give a shit. You're not the first to try and steal my boat and you won't be the last, now get on out of here."

Under the cover of night, it was hard to see the stranger's face. All they could make out was his silhouette.

"Look, we're not trying to steal it. We're just trying to get to my island."

The stranger snorted. "You and the rest of them. Go on, get out of here and don't come back."

Sal turned his flashlight towards the stranger. "Jameson? Jameson McCready, is that you?"

There was a pause for a second. Jameson McCready was a mechanic in town. The name rang a bell but without seeing his face, Frank still wasn't sure who they were dealing with.

"Sal Hudson?"

Sal sighed and flashed Frank a grin. "An old client of mine."

"Ah, I should have figured, let me guess, he suffers from paranoia?" he said before looking back at the wire contraption that had nearly decapitated them.

"What you doing here?" Jameson asked.

"The same thing you are. Trying to stay safe."

"Shouldn't you be at home?"

"Look, it's a long story. You think we can use your boat? I need to get to Frank's island. Gloria is there with the kids and she's not responding to phone calls. And well... Frank's boat isn't at the marina."

Sal started approaching him and Jameson told him to stay back.

"We're not sick, if that's what you're thinking. You?"

He shook his head before peppering them with questions. Where had they been? Had they come in contact with anyone who was ill? Had either of them sniffed, coughed, or felt unwell in the past twenty-four hours? He was skeptical, paranoid even and for good reason. The whole town had succumbed to what other small towns had all over the country. People had got sick, panic had set in, and law and order had got out of control.

"Why is she over there?" Jameson asked.

Sal ran a hand around the back of his neck to work out the tension. Both of them felt as though they were still walking on eggshells with the man.

"I said he could stay there," Frank said. "Safer than being on the mainland."

"That depends."

"What do you mean?"

He snorted again. "Have you two had your head under a rock for the past four days?"

Frank looked at Sal, then back at Jameson. "We've

been out of town."

"Well I guess you can count yourself lucky."

He continued to stare at them but didn't elaborate. It was obvious he was checking out the masks, goggles, and disposable coveralls.

"You got any more of those?"

Frank nodded. "At my cottage. If you want, I'll give you some. Payment for bringing us across."

He sniffed hard. "Sounds fair. You can use the boat, but I'm coming with you. After the shit that I've witnessed in this town, with people acting all crazy, I don't trust anyone. No offense."

"None taken," Sal muttered while making his way up to greet him. He was forgetting all about the six feet of distance he was supposed to keep between him and strangers, so Frank pulled at his jacket before he got too close. Jameson squinted at the bright light Sal was shining in his face. Sal lowered it.

"Keep your distance. Okay?"

Jameson made his way down and moved past them.

Though he had agreed to take them over, it was clear that he wasn't going to trust them. He kept his gun on them at all times even though Sal had asked him to lower it.

The boat bobbed a little as they stepped down into it. Jameson instructed them to stay at the far end. That suited Frank fine. If he had his way, he would have stayed on the dock and let them go by themselves.

The engine roared as he started it up and the boat eased out of the waterfront. Dark water swirled, and a light breeze blew against his face as they made their way toward the island. He swatted a mosquito buzzing at his neck.

"So how's the family?" Sal said trying to break the awkward silence between them. "Meg is dead."

"I'm sorry," Sal replied.

Frank didn't know whether to laugh or cry as the silence settled over them, extra thick this time. Sal went back to staring at the small waves. As they got closer to the island, Frank noticed that none of the lights were on in the house. He glanced at his watch; it was close to nine at night. He figured at least one room would be on.

* * *

Upon arrival, Jameson moored the boat to the dock and they climbed out. Sal didn't wait around, he sprinted for the house with Frank following close behind. When they reached the front door, they found it was locked. Sal looked at him and he fished around in his pockets and then realized the key was with all his other belongings that he'd lost when Chester destroyed his truck.

"Shit!"

Sal banged on the door but there was no answer. They hurried around the back, and tried the rear door but that was locked too.

"Gloria!" Sal shouted but there was no answer. By this point, Jameson had caught up with them and was looking on while keeping his shotgun trained away from them.

"Stand back," Frank said backing up a little. He lunged forward plowing his foot against the door, once, then twice. On the third try it burst open, practically destroying the frame in the process and shattering the glass in the door. Sal went to rush in but Frank grabbed a hold of him and shook his head.

"Hold on." Frank turned to Jameson. "You think I can use your gun?"

He scowled. "The hell you can."

"Well do you want to go in first then?"

"Do I look like a guinea pig?"

Frank was going to make a sarcastic remark but opted to leave it for a more appropriate time. Before he could say he would go in, Sal was already inside calling out her name.

"Gloria!"

He moved further into the five-bedroom cottage until they heard a sound. At first it was barely audible. Muffled even. Sal grabbed the handle to the basement door and edged his way down using the flashlight. He wasn't even thinking whether there was a light switch, he just wanted to see her. Sal reached the bottom of the basement first. Frank heard him gasp as he disappeared out of view. He felt around for the light cord and switched it on. Once

Frank made it down and turned the corner he could see what was going on. Tucked back in the far corner were Gloria and the two kids. There were three mattresses on the ground. None of them were hurt but they looked pretty shaken up. Sal pried a Glock from her hand. Her knuckles had turned white from holding it so tight.

"It's okay, I'm here."

She burst out crying, and his kids clung to him. Frank stared on, and then his eyes drifted around the room. He noticed that the door to the storage room was open and the shelves were empty. *No!* He felt his stomach lurch up into his chest, and his pulse began to race as he darted into the room and took in the sight of what remained. There were a couple of cans of food, enough for a few people to live on for maybe a week at the most. *No. No! What the hell?*

Frank staggered back outside the room and then turned to Gloria who was now beating on Sal for leaving them alone.

"What happened?" Frank asked in a demanding tone.

She wasn't paying attention so Frank went over and grabbed a hold of her arm hard. He wasn't thinking straight and Sal pushed him back.

"Frank!"

"Where has it all gone?" Frank yelled again.

By now Jameson had come down the stairs and he was looking on with wide eyes.

Still shaking, Gloria looked up through tearful eyes. "They took it. All of it."

"Who?"

"Who do you think? The Guthries."

The weight of it crushed down on Frank and churned his stomach. He slipped his hand into his jacket and pulled out his anxiety meds.

"Did they hurt you?" Sal asked, waiting for her to tell him the worst.

She shook her head. "No, but they could have." She beat on his chest with her fist. "We're lucky to be alive because of you." Then she slapped him across the cheek, and did it a second and a third time until Sal stopped her.

"Enough!" He held her tightly and she sobbed into his chest. It was to be expected. It was the reason Frank didn't want Sal to go along with him to Queens. He figured Guthrie wasn't being neighborly when he came by that day. He was scoping the place out. Trying to gauge what security they had. No doubt he saw them leave and waited until they were sure Gloria wasn't a threat before they paid another visit.

Frank went over and scooped up the Glock 22 off the ground and charged towards the stairs. Jameson stepped back as he flew up. He heard Sal say something to Gloria but he wasn't sure what. He was too lost in his anger. When he reached the first floor he went into the kitchen and checked the cupboards. They were completely bare. He slammed his fist into it causing it to give way and break.

"Frank."

Frank pushed past Sal and headed for the back door.

"Don't go over there. You'll get yourself killed."

"If I don't go, we'll die anyway."

Sal caught up with him and grabbed a hold of his arm. "Listen!"

They struggled for a second. "Get off, Sal."

Sal held him by both arms which was a feat for him, Frank could have brushed him off like a fly on any other day.

"We'll get it back. We will. But not now. Now, my wife needs me. My kids need me. And so does yours."

In all the rush to judgment, he had completely forgotten about Ella and the others. He'd become so used to living by himself and relying on no one that it had become second nature. And yet, the moment they entered his mind it only added fuel to the fire. It only served to remind him of what they were lacking. Without food, without a means to keep the place clean, they weren't going to stand a chance.

"You know how long it took me to gather all those things?" Frank yelled.

"Frank. Calm down. If anyone should be mad it's me."

Frank balled his fists and fixed his face towards

Grindstone Island. "I should have known they would do this. Fuck! They took everything we had."

"Listen, go with Jameson, go get the rest of them. I'll stay here with Gloria and when you get back we'll talk about what we can do," Sal said trying his best to calm the situation.

"I know what I'm going to do."

Sal shook his head. "This isn't a war, Frank."

"Sure as hell seems like one."

"We just need a little time to think this one through."

Frank shrugged off Sal's hands. "To hell with thinking it through. You are not going to fix this with your psychobabble. Some men only understand one thing."

"Oh, and you think you are going to waltz over there and get them to give it back. Think logically, Frank."

"I am."

He was boiling inside. He wasn't thinking logically. All he wanted to do was tear Butch's head off his shoulders.

"Breathe, Frank. Breathe."

"Ah to hell with your stupid breathing exercises."

"But they work. Don't they?"

"So does a Glock22 against the side of someone's head." Frank waved the gun around erratically and paced back and forth. The only light that evening came from a crescent moon above them. The gentle sound of waves lapping up against the shore was usually good at lulling Frank into a state of peace but right now, peace was far from his heart. He wanted to fall back on his military training, and right the wrongs, if only because he felt so responsible for allowing Sal to come with him.

"As hard as it might seem, there is an upswing."

"Oh yeah? And what's that?"

"They're alive. Ella is alive, right?" Sal came over to him and patted him on the arm. "We're back now. We can figure this out. Hell, the fact that we managed to survive a trip into the heart of an infected country must count for something."

Frank stood there shaking his head and grinding his teeth. As much as he didn't want to admit it, Sal was right. Once again he was.

"Alright. Stay here. I'll go get the others."

* * *

It felt like a long trip back to the mainland. Jameson was naturally full of questions but Frank wasn't in the right frame of mind to answer. He was thinking of all the ways he was going to make the Guthries pay. He was wrestling with guilt for what Gloria and her kids had been through. Okay, they didn't hurt them but it could have ended much worse. What Butch and his family had done might have been wrong, but it was to be expected now. The nation was facing a threat that could wipe them out with as little as a sneeze, a cough, or a touch. It wasn't hard to imagine that people would look after their own first when faced with hunger and thirst. This was just the tip of the iceberg. Things were going to get even worse and decisions would need to be made. So far he hadn't been put in a situation where he felt like taking someone's life was necessary but he knew if push came to shove, he would do it.

* * *

When the door opened at Sal's home, Hayley answered it. She looked past Frank and frowned. "Where's Sal?"

Her voice carried as the others came out into the hallway and Frank made his way in. Jameson stayed outside. He had a hard job convincing him to let him use the boat again but Frank promised that he'd make it worth his while. In all honesty, he had no idea how he was going to repay him but desperate situations called for great lies. And he was a master at telling them.

Ella frowned. "Dad? What's going on?"

Frank outlined the situation and then instructed them to gather as much of the food, sanitation products, and anything useful they could find from the house. They were going to make a trip over to his apartment as well before they returned to the island.

He decided to not tell them yet about what they had lost, only that Sal was staying with Gloria and the kids until they got back. The last thing he wanted was to make his daughter feel unsafe. The only goal of getting her back to the island was so that he'd have peace of mind and know that however long the virus remained active in the country, they would have a place to stay that was free from disease, hunger, thirst, or those who might seek to harm them. What he hadn't banked on was fighting to get back what was his all along.

At some point in the process of gathering what they could find, Ella pulled her father aside into a quiet room.

"What are you not telling me?"

"Nothing."

"Don't lie, Dad."

"Listen, it's nothing you need to worry about, right now."

"Okay." She placed a hand on her hips and he could tell that she was channeling some of her mother's attitude. "Then answer this. Why did we stop in Lowville? And don't tell me it was just for gas."

"It wasn't. I had to get some supplies."

"Supplies. Right. How come you didn't bring any

back?"

Frank's lip curled up. "They've been teaching you well down at that academy. Nothing gets by you, does it, Ella?"

"Not when it concerns you."

He snorted. As much as he didn't like to keep things from his daughter, the whole incident with Chester was one card he was going to keep close to his chest. It wasn't just the fact that his daughter had been studying to become a police officer, and Chester was one. It was the fact that he didn't want his daughter to perceive him as someone who would stoop as low as Chester had, and yet in reality that's what he had done. Of course, he had never been one for taking his medicine lying down. He also didn't think that he would be seeing Chester again. The guy might have had a few loose screws but if he was telling the truth about having a retreat in upstate New York, no doubt he would be there now, doing what everyone else was — trying to survive.

He never did answer her, though she continued to

badger him.

They collected as much as they could carry and hauled ass back to the boat. On the way over to the island, Frank saw spirals of gray smoke rising from Grindstone Island. They even heard the faint sound of music. He envisioned the Guthries tucking into all the food they had taken, and reveling in the stronghold they had created. Who else had they stolen from? How many others were with them? It didn't matter. They wouldn't be laughing for long.

"Yeah, enjoy it while it lasts, because when I'm done with you, you are going to regret ever having stepped foot on my island," he muttered to himself.

# Chapter 4

That evening the atmosphere in the cottage was solemn. Sal made sure that everyone was settled into the living quarters. Everything Frank envisioned had been turned on its head. It was meant to be just Ella, him, and possibly Kate but that wasn't happening. As he looked around at the other eight, he had begun to wonder how they were going to survive, more specifically how was he going to feed everyone. It felt like it was his responsibility. His burden. They were in his home and all he had to offer was a few cans of beans. What they had taken from Sal's house and his place in Clayton was next to nothing compared to what he'd originally gathered. It would have been tight but at least they could have been able to last a couple of months if they rationed out food and kept it to a bare minimum.

Frank stood in the storage area looking at the empty shelves. They hadn't even left any of his sanitizer. Beyond the one he had in his pocket, and a couple around the house, they had cleaned him out and practically forced him to go cold turkey. He felt like a drug addict without his stash, like an alcoholic without a drop of alcohol left in the house. At least they hadn't found his anxiety medication. On three occasions, he had told his doctor that he'd lost his tablets. Once he told him that an open bottle had fallen into the toilet. All of which meant he was able to get a repeat prescription and stock up on more than was required. He tossed back two tablets and washed them down with a mouthful of water.

The very sound of everyone upstairs made his skin crawl. Sal was right, he had made improvements and with everything that had happened, he was thinking less about his need to repeat his rituals but it wasn't gone entirely. He didn't think it would ever go away entirely. It was a deep-rooted fear and while Sal had helped him to cut the tree back to its roots, the roots spread deep and wide.

"How we doing?" Sal casually leaned against the frame of the door as Frank jotted down on a pad of paper what cans of food the Guthries had left for Gloria and the kids.

"Crazy to think they took everything but left her just enough to get by for a week."

"Maybe he does have a heart," Sal said.

Frank scoffed. "Did you find out from Gloria what they said to her?"

He shook his head. "It's been hard to get a word out of her. She's exhausted. Since they showed up, she's been holed up in the basement with the kids, living on only three or four hours sleep a night." He stepped inside and wiped his finger across the shelves checking for dust. "She's sleeping for now."

"And the kids?"

"Shook up but you know how they are. They bounce back pretty quick."

Frank nodded, and Sal stared at the list. "Why are you writing them down?"

"Well I figure we have about two days' worth of food here. Fortunately, they didn't take the seeds that I had stashed inside a drawer upstairs. But we are going to need food soon."

"What are you going do, Frank?"

"What am I going to do?" He eyed him with a look of confusion. "You mean, what are we going to do? We are all in the same shit hole and it's not getting any brighter down here."

"We are low on guns, ammo, and you can't expect them upstairs to risk their lives."

"You know, under any other conditions I wouldn't ask anyone to do anything but as long as everyone is on this island, they are going to pull their weight. It might not mean firing a weapon, raiding Guthrie's place, or breaking into a store but everyone will be responsible for something. The only way we are going to survive this is by working together."

Frank reached down by a workbench and pulled out a cardboard tube. He popped the plastic lid off the end and emptied out onto the desk a large roll of paper.

"What's that?"

He answered by showing him. He rolled it out across

the top of the desk and laid on top several tins in the corners. It was a map of the islands. It was old and looked outdated as there were some islands listed that no longer existed and a couple that were joined together but had since been divided by the waters.

"We are going to pay Butch a little visit tomorrow evening."

"Frank. This is not some military operation."

Frank stared at him. "Okay, let's play it your way for a second." Frank leaned back against the workbench, amused at the thought of whatever suggestion Sal was going to come up with.

"So? Come on, I'm all ears. This is your chance to have a say."

"I think we should all have a say."

Frank snorted. "Please. You think those kids upstairs are going to have any idea how to approach this? They barely know how to wipe behind their ears."

"Coming from the man who cowered beneath a table, I find that a little insulting."

"Hey! I had a good reason."

"Fear is fear, Frank, and so is courage," he said before pausing. "And besides, not all of them are nineteen like Ella. Zach is twenty."

"Oh really? That makes it all better. One guy who is no longer a teen. Who needs an army when we've got Zach? The kid shot someone and he's still reeling from it. Do you think he's going to pick up a weapon again? We have a better chance of your daughter picking up a gun than him."

"You're not serious, are you? I mean about my daughter."

"Oh god, Sal, get a sense of humor."

Sal hopped up onto the table to take a load off his feet. "So are you suggesting we all just go in there and take it back by force?"

"Do you have a better idea?"

Sal remained quiet for a few seconds.

"They are not going to hand it over," Frank said.

"No… Maybe they won't but it also doesn't mean we

have to take it back from them."

Frank screwed his face up and slapped his hands against the workbench. "If not them, who? You want us to steal from another island the way they stole from us? Is that it?"

"How many of these islands are inhabited all the year around?" Sal asked.

"Not many but let's face it, how many boats were in the harbor? Zero. Which means people are on these islands."

"Not all of them. What I'm saying is the best course of action here might be to just avoid the Guthries. You know, go check out some of the other islands."

"And get our head shot off? How's that any better?"

Sal slipped down off the table. "God sake, Frank, talking to you is like talking to a brick wall. Not everything requires lethal action."

"Did I say we were going to take lethal action?" Frank asked.

"You implied it."

"I said we were going to pay the Guthries a little visit. I didn't say anything about guns."

Sal rubbed his hand across his face. "Talbot, you confuse me more and more every day."

Frank pointed at him. "I like to keep you on your toes."

He smirked. "Trust me, Gloria does that enough. I feel like I'm walking on eggshells with her all day long." He breathed in deeply. "I'm not sure I'm going to make it back from this one."

"Oh she'll come around."

"How do you know?"

"I understand women."

"Right. That's why I'm married and you're divorced." Sal let out a laugh and patted him on the back before heading back upstairs. Frank continued to go over the map. He had visited Grindstone Island on numerous occasions over the years. His earliest memory was when his father took him there. Back then it wasn't as developed as it was today. They had a name for the people who lived there all year around. They called them "Grinders." With the island being the fourth biggest in the Thousand Islands, the best method of getting around was by ATV, something that his father had done when they visited. The island had been full of grassy landscape, two state parks, cattle, barns, and farms, and it was rare to see anyone there except during the summer months. Even in 2016 it still felt like a person was stepping back in time a hundred and fifty years. Seven miles long and three miles wide, the island had provided him with fond memories of lying on Potters Beach and glancing out at boaters as they anchored to sunbathe.

Perhaps that's why his grandparents had purchased the island he was on now. Its close proximity to Grindstone allowed them to enjoy both the beauty of the island and the privacy of their own.

Not long after Frank had met Kate, he wanted her to live there all year around but she wouldn't do it. She wanted the stability that came from living on the mainland, being close to stores without having to hop into a boat.

Frank was still lost in thought when Sal returned. "Oh Frank, I forgot to tell you. Gloria said they took the boat as well."

"Of course they did."

Sal tapped the side of the door frame and disappeared. A few minutes later Gabriel and Tyrell appeared.

"Okay to come in?"

He inhaled deeply from behind his mask, did a quick once-over check in his mind, then counted back from ten. "Sure, come in."

"Quite a place you got here. You own the island?"

"Yeah."

"So Sal was telling us about the problem. You're going to pay them a visit?"

"Right."

"Anything we can do to help?"

"I wouldn't ask—"

"Hey, look, Mr. Talbot, we appreciate what you have done for us so far. We'd like to pull our weight. I'm not one for leeching off anyone. If there is anything we can do, just let me know," Gabriel said.

He nodded but was reluctant to get them involved in an issue that was between the Guthries and him. But that's when it dawned on Frank.

Butch knew Sal and Ella, but not these guys.

Frank leaned back on the bench. "Perhaps there is something you can do."

"Just say the word."

He got this grin on his face. "How good are you at swimming?"

## Chapter 5

The next morning, Frank awoke to a warm band of light covering his face. It had been a long while since he'd slept so well. With more than enough space in the house, he was glad that he didn't have to give up his bed. Fortunately no one was interested in taking it. Sal, Gloria, and the kids slept in the two guest rooms beside his, Hayley and Ella took the other rooms and the three lads used the living room.

Before they went to sleep that night, he'd made a point to find out who had fired a weapon. Those who hadn't he would teach as soon as they got some more. That was one of the first things on his to-do list that morning. Though he had told Sal that he wasn't planning on using force to get back what belonged to him, he was also realistic about the fact that Guthrie wasn't going to hand over what they had without some resistance.

While lying in bed, chewing over what he had to get

done, he heard the guttural sound of a boat's engine. At first he thought it was just passing by, then it got louder. Expecting it to be the Guthries, he bolted out of bed, tossed the sheets across the room and went over to the window. With the thick canopy of hemlock, cedar, and pine trees blocking his view of the boathouse, he couldn't tell who it was. Not wasting a minute, he rushed downstairs without a thought for what he had on. All he was wearing was a pair of white boxer shorts, and silver dog tags on a chain around his neck.

"Tyrell, where's the Glock?"

He rubbed his eyes and tried to wake up. The moment he caught sight of Frank in boxer shorts he backed up. "Mr. T., I'm not into that shit."

"No, you idiot. Where's the gun? I need it."

"Oh, uh, it's over there," he said pointing to the small coffee table across the room.

He shook his head in bewilderment. The fact that he had been able to get this close to Tyrell without waking him meant he could have snatched that gun off the table and shot them all before they even knew he was there. Things would have to change around here if they were going to stay. Frank gave a quick check to make sure the magazine was loaded and he bolted out the front door. He dropped to one knee on the porch and waited for them to show their faces. He could hear boots trudging up along the small paved pathway. When the figure came around the corner he lowered his gun, and breathed a sigh of relief.

"Jameson, you scared the shit out of me."

"Likewise. Nice shorts," he said with a smirk on his face. "You might want to put something on."

He'd forgotten that Jameson had returned home the previous evening.

Following close behind him was his daughter. She couldn't have been more than eight years of age. Jameson placed a hand over her eyes but she pushed around to see what all the fuss was about. When she caught sight of him, she started to giggle.

"Oh, right. Yeah. Um." He suddenly became very

conscious of the fact that he was barely covered up. His cheeks went beet red. He slipped back inside then poked his head out again.

"Actually, why are you here?"

He held up a wicker basket. "I brought breakfast. Thought you folks could use some extra food."

His eyebrows shot up and he darted back inside to get some clothes on. By now Sal was up and coming down the stairs as Frank was rushing up.

"I always took you for a briefs man, Frank." Sal smiled.

"Shut it."

He passed by Gloria on the way to his room and he went from running like a kid trying to cover up his nakedness to ambling into his room with all the pride of a lion. Five minutes later he came down feeling more like himself and little less embarrassed. The others had welcomed Jameson in without even a second thought to the fact that he or his daughter could be infected. Frank stood across the room from them all with a look of concern on his face. This time, however, it was Jameson that stepped forward to alleviate his worries.

"She's not sniffed, coughed, or been anywhere near her mother in over a month. I had sole custody of her."

"That's comforting to know. By the way, why were you a client of Sal's? Paranoia?"

Sal stood behind Jameson making a swiping motion across his lips as if he didn't want Frank to say anything.

Jameson turned slightly and smiled. "Is that what you told him, Sal?"

Sal threw his hands up. "No. Patient confidentiality prevents me."

"It was just my guess, you know, with the whole trap thing you had set up back at the dock."

Jameson chuckled. "I was seeing him about my wife."

Frank rolled his eyes. "Aren't we all!"

"Anyway, let's get this breakfast going." He turned and carried the basket full of food into the kitchen. The others followed and Sal placed a hand over his face unable to believe what Frank had said.

"What? You said he was a client."

"Dear god," Sal muttered as they went in to prepare some breakfast. That morning was the first of what would become many days together. Though they had been drawn together under the strangest of circumstances, Frank could already sense something was beginning to form between them all. Family? Friendship? The last time he had felt anything like that was from his days in the military.

They laughed and chatted around the breakfast table that morning, and for a brief moment they almost forgot that the world outside had changed. It was the sudden sound of a gun going off that snapped them back into the present fear. Frank jumped to his feet and rushed to the window. There was no one outside. He opened the window just as a second one went off. This time he could tell where it was coming from — Grindstone Island.

* * *

Butch Guthrie felt as though he was being more than generous by allowing some of the homeowners on the island to stay in exchange for them giving up what they had. Since the shit storm of the century had kicked off, he had been hedging his bets and strategically preparing for what was coming down the pipeline — martial law.

Of course he didn't expect that now. Not after the breaches. Not after the huge loss of life throughout the country. Not after the virus had reached Clayton. No one was going to stick his or her neck out on the line, working for the government for a measly paycheck. Hell, there was no one left to cut the checks. The disbanding of the police in Clayton had been proof of that. Sure, there were a few that thought they were going to continue to uphold the law, but they soon came around to his way of thinking when faced with the reality that their colleagues had decided on survival over duty.

He'd said it countless times in the prepper retreats. People will toe the line only for so long. When push came to shove, when a man got squeezed into a corner, you would truly see what they were made of.

Butch walked back and forth around the next family

that had shown up on the island. He'd been through six other families just like them. He'd already fired two shots in the air as a warning to them but they still didn't seem to be getting the point. He even brought over the Bolmer family and had them explain it, thinking that might save them from what he was going to do if they continued to cause trouble.

"Look, it's pretty simple. Whatever you have now belongs to us. If you wish to leave the island, you can. I'm not here to bully you. Let's get that straight."

Tom Hannigan, the father and husband of the Hannigan family, stepped forward. He was a short stocky man wearing a pressed red and white striped shirt. He was the very kind of people that Butch despised. A Harvard type. Well educated. More money than sense. They were the kind of people that would fork out cash for the biggest boat, the largest house and put on snooty cocktail parties but when it came to survival they didn't know shit. But what pissed him off even more than that was the fact they still thought they had the right to tell him what to do.

"You're not a bully? What the hell do you think barging into our home and robbing us is?"

Butch could see that he was seething. He loved it. This was what he lived for. Seeing the very people that had relied on the government, who had turned their nose up at his family, trying to act all brave and shit.

"It's called taking charge. Someone's got to do it."

"And who put you in charge? From what I can tell this is still a free country, we own this property and pandemic or not, you have no right to take what belongs to us."

Butch snorted and looked at his brothers, Dougie and Bret. They, along with his cousins Joey and Dusty and their wives formed an arc around the family who had been marched outside. Of course, Tom would disagree. In his mind, they were dragged. Manhandled. Hell, even pistol-whipped. The guy was a wimp.

Butch leaned in. "No right? Belongs to you? I'm going to take what you just said as a misunderstanding on your part. Perhaps you didn't look over the fine print when you purchased the property, or maybe you are just ignorant of the history of this island. So, I'm going to let that one slide. Let me tell you a few things. This island doesn't belong to you. That property doesn't belong to you. Everything on this island was once owned by my family."

"Maybe so, but that was before your family sold land. I have the deed to this place. It's mine. By law, I have rights and right now you are infringing upon those rights."

"Um. Oh, I do love a good speech. Well, please by all means — call the cops. In fact, let me do it for you."

Butch reached into his pocket and pulled out his cell phone and dialed 911. He mimicked the sound of the dial tone.

"Ah yes, operator, I need police assistance." He paused and smiled. "Oh, what's that? You want me to wait. Oh, no problem. Sure, go ahead. Take your time."

He whistled and his brothers and cousins chuckled. All of them were holding AR-15s. He walked closer to Tom and then stopped right in front of him.

"Sherriff? Butch Guthrie here, I have a little bit of a discrepancy over land rights. What's that? You'll come right out? Oh great, I can't wait for you to get here." He paused. "Tom Hannigan. That's right. You want to speak to him? Okay, let me put him on the line."

Butch handed the phone to Tom. He took a step back and looked at him cautiously. He was hesitant to take it but Butch told him to take it. He took the phone and put it up to his ear.

"Sheriff?"

When there was no answer, Butch burst out laughing. "The sheriff isn't coming because there is no police department operating, you moron. Now give me that." Butch snatched the phone from Tom's feeble hand. It was like taking a toy from a baby.

Clayton Police Department only consisted of three full-time officers and two part-timers. They hardly ever dealt with crime. And with a pandemic breathing down their neck, none of them were in a position to deal with the fires or the looting or public outcry. Fear took care of that. Of course, Butch was grateful. It meant he didn't have to waste a bullet.

"Then the National Guard," Tom blurted.

"Look around you. Do you hear choppers overhead? Did you see any military in the town on your way here? No. That's because they are swamped and a shitty little town in the armpit of nowhere is the last place on their list."

Tom swallowed hard and looked over to his wife and two kids who looked as if they had just stepped out of prep school. Their clothes screamed high fashion. Their view about life was privilege and rights; the kind of people that probably never worked a goddamn day in their whole life.

"The only law and rules that exist now are the ones I make." He stared at Tom, studying him. He cast a glance at his wife, a dolled-up blonde with a tight ass that matched her face. "Don't look at me as though I'm the bad guy here. I'm doing a good thing."

A look of confusion spread across his brow. "What, by

taking everything we have?"

"I'm not taking everything. Just the essentials. We'll leave you with some things to get by, the rest you will get once you chip in and help."

"Chip in and help?"

Butch snorted. "Oh, that's right. You self-indulgent assholes don't understand the meaning of help. You like to be waited on. I bet you book a reservation even if the restaurant doesn't take reservations. I bet you buy the most expensive wine just so you can say how expensive it is." He let out a chuckle as he stepped closer.

Tom put up a finger and staggered back. "Don't touch me."

"Tom. Tom. Relax, no one is going to touch anyone around here. Like I said. I'm not the bad guy here. But if we are going to ride this out, and you are going to be here on the island, there are some rules you have to follow."

"Why do you need to make them?"

"Are you making them? Huh? Or how about your little wifey here? Pretty little thing she is."

He stepped forward showing all the courage of a mouse. "Back away from her."

"Or what?" Butch smiled. "What are you gonna do?" He waited to see but Tom just looked nervous. "That's right. You are going to keep your trap shut and your ears open. Believe me, once this is over, you'll thank me."

"You're insane."

"All the best ones are. Joey, Dusty, head on in and lighten their load."

"You got it, Butch."

They pressed on towards the house. A look of dismay, horror or shock came over the Hannigans. All they could do was stand and watch with their mouths open. That was until Tom decided to grow a pair.

He moved forward and grabbed a hold of Butch by the arm. "I'm telling you…"

Before he could get another word of out his mouth, Butch threw a hook and cracked him on the jaw. Tom stumbled back and collapsed to the ground. His wife and kids rushed to his side and looked on in horror.

"Now, I didn't want to do that." He wagged his finger at him. "But you forced my hand. You're lucky if I leave you anything. I could throw you off this island, drown you, put a bullet in your skulls but I'm not going to do that. You and your nice little family here are going to be safe because of me. So, if you want a reason for why I'm taking all this… Call it payment, protection money. As long as you are on this island, no harm will come to you. You'll be safe from sickness and safe from anyone who tries to take what you have. I think that's fair. Don't you?"

Tom spat some blood on the ground. His bottom lip was cut. He didn't reply. He wouldn't. He didn't have the balls to. They cowered on the ground and his wife looked as if she was going to say something but Tom pulled at her arm.

"Of course, the alternative is simple. You get the fuck off my island!" He glared at him. "You decide."

One by one his cousins came out with boxes of goods and loaded them onto the back trailers hooked up to

ATV's. All the while Butch sat by, smoking a cigarette. He gazed around at the island with a deep sense of pride. It had been years since his family had owned the entire island. Honestly, he wasn't too sure at what point the property changed hands. The Evertson family had originally purchased it back in 1831 for a measly $15,000. They had owned it for forty years. At some point between then and now, the Guthrie family purchased it; at least that's what his grandfather had told him. Whether it was true or not, mattered little to him. But, he took his grandfather at his word. He wasn't a man to lie. And he would challenge anyone who refuted his claim. At some point, parts of the island were sold off leaving a large section of private property on the west side. That still belonged to them, but the rest was up for grabs and rich folk looking to impress friends had snapped it up.

The ATV's roared to life and tore away, leaving huge muddy ruts in the front of Tom's yard. Before Butch left he shouted over his shoulder. "Oh, we plan to hold weekly meetings over at Dodge Hall. I expect you to be there. And if you're religious, you can use the Methodist church across the street from the community center. All tithes go to me."

He let out a chuckle and pulled away with his girlfriend Misty on the rear seat.

# Chapter 6

Butch Guthrie felt like a king back at the farm. The home itself was over 7,000 square feet, made of pine and fir flooring. In his opinion it had one of the best views of river, meadowlands, and beach. With nine bedrooms, three fireplaces, and four full bathrooms it had more than enough space for his family.

For years, they had been inviting people out to the island to get ready for the big one, and now that it had hit, where were they? Most of the people that signed up for his retreats came from all over the United States. Smart folk. People he would have gladly shared his home with, the kind of people he could have used.

While he had his brothers and cousins with him, several other families who had lived in Clayton joined him there. Trustworthy, hard-working, and loyal. Each of them had gone through his course and were willing to do whatever it took to survive. With close to twenty of them ready to fight at the drop of a hat, he felt safe sleeping at night and calling the shots on the island.

Though his brother Bret was worried that cops would eventually show up, he didn't have any doubt in his mind about how things would play out. Within the first forty-eight hours after folks in Clayton started to become infected and die, he knew it wasn't going to get any better.

While he wouldn't have thought twice about putting a slug in a cop's head, he wasn't going to jump the gun on this one. Misty had kept him in check and made sure that he stayed level-headed. That was the only reason he hadn't resorted to violence. But he would if anyone got out of line.

He breathed in deeply the salty air and looked out across the lush green landscape, taking in the sight of his kingdom. That's exactly how he saw it. He'd always resented the fact that he had to share the island with others. He'd considered getting a smaller plot of land, like some of his friends, and Frank Talbot, but there was something about the history of Grindstone that he loved.

Butch snorted at the thought of Talbot. What a pathetic sight that was. Leaving Gloria alone. That one had been too easy. In fact, he was impressed at what they had managed to haul away from the property. Compared to some of the idiots living on this island, he made their storage units look pathetic. In some ways, he kind of regretted taking all that he had from him. Not that he'd mention it to anyone. Staying in control, or at least giving the perception that he was in control was important.

He smirked, relishing the thought of Gloria's face. The shock. The surprise.

Butch sipped on his cold beer, while sitting comfortably in an Adirondack chair and basking in what he had established. His thoughts drifted back to his visit.

*"Hello, Gloria."*

*"Let go of my kids."*

*He shifted from one foot to the next and put his hand out. "Now, now settle down. No one is going to get harmed." He* grinned. "Where's Sal? Frank?"

"They've gone into town. They'll be back soon, so you better let my kids go or I'll…"

She lunged forward but Dougie grabbed a hold of her hair and she let out a scream.

"Oh now, be gentle with her, Dougie. We aren't here to harm anyone." He glanced around suspiciously. "So what did they go to get?"

She shrugged. "Supplies."

"Really?"

She nodded.

He eyed her. The way her eyes shifted back and forth. "You're not very good at lying, are you, Gloria?"

"What do you want?" she spat back.

"What do you think?"

Gloria smoothed out her outfit and Butch chuckled. "Please. Gloria, I'm not that desperate. Where's the storage area?"

When she didn't reply, he got real close to her and ran a cupped hand over her cheek, down her neck, and across her *breast. She grimaced at his touch.*

*He leaned in and spoke quietly in her ear. "Don't make me ask again."*

*"Down in the basement."*

*He gave a nod to Bret and Misty and they headed down to start gathering whatever they could find. Butch sucked air between his teeth, pulled out a cigarette, and lit it. He blew some smoke near Gloria's face just to irritate her. She was such a prissy little bitch. How the hell Sal put up with her was beyond him. He often overheard him chatting to Frank about her when they visited the store. That was part of the reason he never put a ring on Misty's finger. Marriage fucked things up. Changed the dynamics of the relationship. It made people go crazy and think they could do whatever the hell they wanted. It gave people a sense of entitlement. Nah, he wasn't playing those games. As long as he had a warm bit of ass at the end of the night, that was all he cared about.*

*Bret soon returned bearing gifts. He raised up several bags of rice, and bags of potatoes.*

*"Seriously, Butch. You should go see what this crazy*

*fucker has got. He has more hand sanitizer than a sex shop. We hit the mother lode on this one."*

*He flashed a toothy grin to Gloria before taking another puff on his cigarette.*

*"You're making a big mistake," Gloria said. Dougie had a tight grip on her arm and still she struggled to get loose. Butch nodded to him.*

*"It's okay, Dougie, let her go."*

*She went to move towards her children but he put his hand up, and made a tutting sound.*

*"What about weapons?"*

*She shook her head.*

*"Are you telling me they left you all alone without a weapon?"*

*"We didn't expect assholes like you to show up."*

*Butch bit on the bottom of his lip while studying her face. "How about I let Dougie here take you outside and show you some manners?"*

*Dougie started chuckling. "Yeah, let me do that, Butch." He reached over and grabbed her by the ass. She spun around* and tried to hit him but he pushed her back. Butch went to intervene but she spat in his face and began yelling.

"You come in here and lay hands on my children. You take what doesn't belong to you. You're all cowards."

Slowly, Butch wiped his cheek and then licked the back of his hand to taste her spit. "Sweet."

In an instant, he lashed out and slapped her across the cheek and she fell to the floor. She started sobbing. Her kids began to cry but Joey and Dusty held them back.

Butch loomed over her and wagged his finger in her face. "Show some respect. Your old man might not stand up to you but I sure as hell will."

Cowering on the floor gripping her cheek she yelled back. "And that makes you a man? Hitting a woman. Scaring children."

He squinted and grinned, then wagged his finger in the air. "See, that's what I like about you, Gloria. You don't give an inch. I can see why Sal walks around with his balls in his purse. You wear the pants, don't you?"

"Fuck you."

*He shook his head. Then just like that he breathed in deeply and smiled. "Come now. Let's get you up and cleaned off. This is going to be over very soon but let's not have any more disrespect. I won't tolerate it." As he helped her up, an image of his own father doing the same thing to his mother and saying the very same words briefly flashed across his mind.*

*She shot back. "When Sal gets back, you're—"*

*Butch gripped her arm tight and cut her off. "Yeah?"*

*She swallowed her tears, her lip quivered, and she looked as if she was about to say something. Her face was red and her hair a tattered mess. He smoothed it out and she tried to back away from his touch.*

*"Right, boys, haul it out. And let the woman have her children back."*

The sound of Bret's voice snapped him out of the past.

"Butch, can I speak with you for a moment?"

Bret was the youngest in the family. At twenty-eight years of age he was still very wet behind the ears and it didn't take much to worry him. Ever since they had arrived, he had been trying to get an answer as to why they needed to take from others when they had more than enough.

"Sure."

Butch got up, carrying his beer into the greenhouse.

It was true. They didn't need the extra supplies. For years, his family had been storing away all the essentials that were needed to survive the worst-case scenario. Beneath the farmhouse was a bunker that could protect them from a nuclear attack. They had weapons buried all around the property, and more than enough food to feed their family for at least two years without having to scavenge. The property had several backup generators that could be powered by the sun or by fuel. On the land they had multiple greenhouses for growing their own produce. The major one that they had just stepped into was on the side of the home. It didn't even look like a greenhouse. It was made to look like an enclosed porch. It produced five times the amount of food that a regular hoop greenhouse could offer and would grow food all year round. It didn't rely on fertilizer or pesticides and would allow them to grow citrus or coffee trees if they wanted. There was even an area for incubating chickens and ducks.

The way he saw it, if there was going to be a shortage of food, he sure as hell wasn't going to suffer.

"So, what's on your mind?"

He looked agitated. "Look, I've been thinking." He paced up and down a little.

"Shit, Bret, have you been taking LSD or something?"

"I don't like this. Not one bit."

"What don't you like?" Butch said, leaning against the doorframe.

"This, taking people's supplies. They have a right to survive and fend for themselves."

"And they will."

He shrugged. "So why are we taking them?"

Butch scoffed, and placed his arm around his brother. "Bret, you're not seeing the bigger picture here. Let me lay it out for you. How long do you think it's going to be before people come knocking on our door asking for handouts? How long do you think it's going to be before they show up with guns, demanding that we hand over what we have? And I'm not just talking about food and water. Look around you. All of this is a gold mine to the desperate. And believe me, people are going to be desperate. They already are."

"But you're just speeding up that process by taking away what they do have."

"This isn't about taking supplies from people. It's much more than that. It's establishing a position. Drawing a line in the sand before people get desperate. It allows them to know that we aren't going to be fucked with, and let's face it, the crops we'll have to produce aren't going to tend themselves. We are going to have to do it. Do you want to do it?"

Bret got this nervous look on his face. "I... I don't get it."

He sighed. Trying to get through to him was like speaking to a wall. He was sure he'd been adopted.

"Look at it this way. Why isn't everyone rich in the world? Huh? I mean, it would be simple to print off money and distribute it out to individuals. You know... level out the playing field and all. Make sure that everyone has an equal share. But why doesn't that happen?"

He shrugged.

"Who would do anything? Who would make food? Who would do all the shitty jobs that no one else wants to do in the world? No one would do it, if they already had everything they needed. It's motivation. Simply logic. Come on, walk with me," Butch said leading him outside again and down to the water's edge. The waves frothed round the rocks and a breeze blew in. He gazed out across the dark waters towards the island that Frank Talbot owned. He considered what they had done to him.

"If everyone holds the keys to the kingdom, there is no need for a king, no need for servants, no need for rules to be followed. Everyone would call the shots. Do you know how out of control that would get?"

"But people would step up. You know, help each other out."

He squeezed gently the back of his neck. "And we're doing that, brother."

Bret screwed up his face. "By taking what they have?"

"By distributing it out fairly. We're not keeping it all to ourselves. How do I put this? We're just holding it, like a deposit. Once we see people listening, following directions, and carrying their weight, they will be taken care of. You have my word. And you know about my word, right?"

"It's your bond."

He chuckled. "That's a good lad. You're catching on."

Butch pulled out his cigarettes and offered Bret one. He took it and both of them stood there looking out across the water to Clayton.

"You think mother and father would have approved of this?"

"You can bet your ass on it. Hell, father wouldn't have treated Tom Hannigan the way I did. That man is lucky to still be alive."

Bret nodded. "So how are you going to do this? I mean, some of those folks who are staying don't have enough in their cupboards now."

"Don't you worry about that. We will discuss it at the first town hall meeting."

Bret scoffed. "You really think people are going to show up to that after what we just did?"

Butch replied instantly. "If they want to survive they will. C'mon, let's go."

He put his arm around his brother's shoulder and started leading him back. He had only gone a few feet when he heard the distant sound of a boat engine. Butch glanced over his shoulder and squinted. He cupped a hand over his eyes to block out the morning sun.

There was a boat coming from Frank Talbot's island.

"Huh!"

"What is it?" Bret asked.

He continued squinting for a moment as he watched the boat head for the mainland. Had Frank returned or was it someone else?

Butch shook his head slowly. "I don't know yet but I'm going to find out."

## Chapter 7

The water was choppy on the way over to the marina. Frank had left the others on the island while he and Jameson returned to Clayton to see what firearms they could find. There was a store in town but Jameson said that it was one of the first places to be looted. Seemed everyone had the same idea. Gear up and get ready for the worst.

"What did your wife do?" Frank asked.

Jameson gripped the wheel a little harder, making his knuckles go white.

"She was a teacher. She taught eighth-grade kids."

He fixed his face like a flint and the boat burst over a set of solid waves forcing Frank back in his seat. For a small boat it could move surprisingly fast. A light mist hit their faces. The crisp morning air opened up his lungs, and for a few minutes he thought about Kate.

"What did you tell your daughter about your wife?"

"The truth. We've always been honest with each other. She's a good kid."

"I couldn't help but notice that she doesn't look like you."

"That's right. I'm her stepfather. She still refers to me as her father. The real one ran off with some girl seven years ago. Piece of work he was."

Frank nodded and popped an anxiety tablet into his mouth. Jameson noticed and for a short while, he could tell he was biting at the bit to pepper him with questions.

"So you were seeing Sal?"

Frank was hesitant to respond. "Yeah, unfortunately."

"I don't know… he helped me."

"What did you have?"

"Trouble in my marriage, stress and whatnot."

"With Meg?"

"No, my ex."

"Oh, you have one too."

Jameson gave him a sideways glance. "Yeah, Sal said you were divorced."

"What else did he tell you?"

"You tend to go a little crazy when you don't get your meds."

He snorted. "Well he isn't wrong about that. But it's gotten better."

"You sure?"

"I haven't had much choice. This whole upheaval has been like a baptism by fire." He paused for a second. "You sure this guy has weapons?"

"They might be illegal and we're liable to get our head shot off but, yeah, if you win him over I'm sure he'll hook us up."

"Us?"

Jameson cleared his throat. "You seem to have something going here with the island and all. I've been cooped up inside that house just waiting for them to show up."

"By them you mean?"

"You know, the looters, home invaders, the Guthries."

Frank leaned in a little. "You've seen them?"

"Oh, yeah, I saw them. A few days ago heading into town, starting fires."

Frank let out a heavy sigh.

"You are going to have your work cut out for you if you're thinking of going over and causing trouble."

"I'm not going to cause trouble."

"No? So the guns are just for looks?"

Both of them smirked.

"So your ex, she local?"

"She was. We had a little boy together. Marcus. He's fifteen now. They live in Watertown with her new guy. I don't get to see him though. Yep, she made that quite clear."

"Must be hard."

He sighed. "It is but what can you do? I'd considered going through the courts but it would have been a waste of time. She would have just upped and disappeared. At least having her in Watertown I could drive by every now and again and see him from a distance."

"He didn't want to know you?"

"She wouldn't let him. In his mind, I abandoned her."

He raised an eyebrow. "And yet she went off with another guy?"

"Yeah."

"Sorry to hear that."

"Ah it's alright. She was a crackhead anyway. Nothing like Meg."

"So where did you meet Meg?"

"At a singles night, believe it or not. Yeah. I lucked out with her. Gorgeous girl. Dark hair, perfectly blue eyes, and a figure that would make your head turn. Her last guy used to hit her. If I could have got my hands on him I would have... Anyway, I don't know what she saw in me but I was glad to have known her. Even if it was for just a short time."

His eyes dropped slightly and it was clear that his mind was elsewhere.

There was an awkward silence between them. "So this guy, with the weapons. How long you have known him?"

"A long while. Let's just say he owes me a favor."

"So why do I need to win him over?"

"Because I owe him several. He'll probably be nicer to you."

The boat started getting closer to the dock, which backed onto his property. He killed the engine and brought it in slowly. Frank tossed the rope and then hopped up onto the dock and tied it off. Once Jameson was out he reengaged his trap and covered up the boat with branches.

"Where did you learn to make stuff like that?"

"I'm a mechanic. Let's just say I don't work on cars in my off time."

Frank regarded him with amusement. "So you build traps in your spare time, and you're taking me to see some dubious guy who is liable to blow our heads off. You want to run by me what you do again?"

He grinned and they headed up the steep incline to his house to get his truck and head over to the stranger's home.

"What's the guy's name?"

"Abner Rooney."

"Let's hope he's still alive."

Frank hopped in the other side of the truck and the engine growled to life. "Oh, he's alive. If you think Butch Guthrie is mentally unstable, you wait until you meet Abner."

Frank raised an eyebrow. "Great. He's not related, is he?"

## Chapter 8

Abner Rooney lived at the end of a gravel driveway just off Cottage Road, in the north end of Clayton. He owned a boat restoration business. A large American flag was flapping in the wind outside his property. Next to his stone house was a long, rustic blue clapboard building that Jameson said was used for his business. As they got closer to his property, Frank noticed that the inside of the lot was full of large schooners in various states of decay. A steel chain-link fence wrapped around the property and a large sign on the front of the gate warned people to beware of the dog.

"How do you know this guy again?"

"Before I got taken on full-time at Jim's garage, I used to work for him. He does a little of everything. Restoration of boats and vehicles. He has a small wrecker's yard out back. Guy has had me create some weird mechanical contraptions in his house. You want to meet someone who is paranoid. This is the guy."

"And he definitely has guns?"

They parked in front of the gate. "Oh yeah, you just wait and see what I built him for his little stash. But remember, he's a little skittish."

"What does he need them for?"

"He collects mostly but he enjoys hunting."

"So he knows the Guthries?"

"Who doesn't?"

Frank pushed out of the truck and made his way down to the gate. There was a small chain and cow bell on the far side. Jameson swung it back and forth and it let out a clattering sound that reverberated around.

"Abner, you there?" Jameson hollered.

A few minutes passed without any response and then gunfire erupted. Several bursts and Jameson and Frank hit the ground and started scrambling back towards the truck on their bellies.

"I told you he's a bit skittish."

"Holy shit. Maybe we should just forget this."

"Your call. But I can tell you there are no guns left at the gun shop in town. It's been cleaned out."

Frank sought cover behind the truck door and peered out. "You got your shotgun?"

"You don't want to show that. He will drop you before you get within spitting distance. Guy was in Vietnam, a sniper."

"Can't be a good shot."

"Oh, he is. Those were warning shots. If he wanted you dead, you'd be gone by now."

"Comforting," Frank replied.

Jameson grinned. "Abner, it's me, Jameson."

A grizzly voice called out. "Come out with your hands where I can see 'em."

"Is he serious?"

"Just do what he says," Jameson replied as he edged his way out and shuffled over to the gate. The sign on the front was hanging by a single piece of wire. Everything about the place looked run-down. To think that anyone brought their business here was ludicrous.

"That's far enough," a hard voice bellowed over a speaker that was installed on a tree off to the left. By now he had expected to see some terrifying looking Rottweilers or Dobermans chewing at the fence but there were none.

"Where's his dog?"

"You're listening to it. They nicknamed him Dog when he was in the army. The sign on the gate was a gift from his brother. Some kind of birthday joke. He used to say he was going to take it down but he never bothered."

Frank scowled. Clayton was full of nutcases. After living there his entire life, he thought he had met them all — obviously not.

Abner hollered again. "And where's your weapons?"

"That's actually why we are here," Jameson replied.

"You expect me to believe you aren't carrying?"

"I have my shotgun in the truck, but Frank here wants to talk to you about getting a gun or two."

"Frank who?"

Frank stepped closer. "Talbot."

"Never heard of you."

"Terry Talbot's boy," Frank replied.

"Doesn't ring a bell."

"Rachael Talbot."

"Talbot," Abner muttered with a voice that sounded like he'd smoked one too many cigarettes. "Did she run a convenience store?"

Frank glanced at Jameson. "That's it."

"Um. Nope. Don't know her."

Frank palmed his face. Jameson edged forward. "Listen, you old coot, open up the gate."

"Did you bring my money?"

"No, did you bring mine?" Jameson replied, then his lip curled up.

"Don't be coy with me, boy. If you don't have my money, I don't have any time for you."

Frank leaned over to Jameson. "How much do you owe him?"

"Twenty-five hundred. But he owes me over six grand for work I did over a period of six months. Every time I would bring it up, he would say his memory wasn't what it used to be. But oh, he could remember me owing him money. As far as I'm concerned we are even and he still owes me at least three and a half."

"I can hear you!" Abner hollered in a gruff voice.

"Then you know that we are even in regards to money."

"Bullshit. I might be getting old but I ain't stupid."

Frank had enough of this going back and forth. It wasn't getting them anywhere. "Mr. Rooney. I'll give you the twenty-five hundred he owes you, and more if you have guns for sale. Just let us in."

There was near silence for a few minutes. All that could be heard was the river, and a flock of birds that broke in the trees.

"How can I be sure you aren't trying to get in here and steal what I have?"

"I told you. He's not going to let us in," Jameson said turning and heading back to the truck. Frank, though, hadn't come this far to get turned down.

"Because we don't have any weapons on us except the

one in the truck."

"How can I be sure?"

"Well, I guess you'll have to take my word for it."

"I wish I could but unfortunately, your word means shit to me boy. Besides, you could have that virus. I think I'm safer staying clear of you."

"We are masked up. No symptoms in over seventy-two hours."

Again, more silence. Frank sighed. "Look, you tell me what you want us to do and we'll do it."

As quick as a heartbeat he responded. "Strip."

Frank nearly coughed up a lung. "Excuse me?"

"Strip down. Only way I can be sure you ain't got guns."

Jameson rushed over to the speaker and started yelling. "Screw that. You crazy old coot! It's not happening."

"Then have a good day and piss off."

Frank stared down at the gravel ground beneath him. He had done a lot of crazy things in his time to get what he wanted but the idea of stripping off topped them all.

Still in a crouched position and peering through the fence, he could see a gun barrel sticking out of a metal door. There was small grill and the barrel was shoved into the opening and kept moving around.

Frank went over to Jameson who was leaning against the fence and tugged at him. "We could go around the side, jump the fence, and break in."

"Are you out of your mind? This guy probably has the place rigged up by now with all manner of traps."

"How would you know?"

"Because I made the damn things."

Ah, things were starting to fall into place. He obviously wasn't just seeing Sal about his marriage. The guy was insane. Frank stood there for a moment before he began taking off his jacket and undoing his shirt.

Jameson frowned. "What are you doing?"

"It's the only way in."

"You are playing into his head games," Jameson said.

"Maybe. But if it gives him peace of mind and gets us those guns, let's just do it."

Jameson was hesitant at first. He scowled like a kid who was being forced to eat his greens. "Damn old coot."

Slowly they undressed until they were down to their underpants.

"Satisfied?"

"That's real nice. Take 'em off."

"What?" Jameson hollered back.

"Don't make me repeat myself. Take 'em off."

A warm breeze brushed against Frank's skin and he was beginning to question doing this. But they had gone this far. He whipped off his underpants and then stood there covering up his privates with his clothes. Jameson did the same thing.

"Alright, last thing. Drop the clothes in front of you and squat."

What the hell was this? A prison strip search? An annual physical? Frank dropped his and cupped his balls and squatted down.

"Cough."

He coughed.

"Like we are really going to stash a Glock up our asses, you bastard," Jameson said. A roar of laughter came back over the speaker. It was uncontrollable and it made both of them realize they were being made to look like fools. Frank went to put his clothes on and the laughter stopped.

"What are you doing?" Abner said.

"Well it's a joke, right? This whole thing was a joke..."

"I wasn't laughing at you boneheads. I was laughing at a movie I'm watching. You can leave your clothes there, put your underpants back on, and bring in the money."

They looked at each other dumbfounded.

A buzzing sound was heard and the gate screeched back either side. They stood there for a minute contemplating what other hoops this guy was going to make them jump through. Frank slipped his underpants on, fished out the wad of money from in his jacket, and headed on in. Jameson caught up with him.

"Where did you get all that money from?"

"Withdrew it from the bank before this shit storm

happened. Better question is, why does he want with it? It's no use to him."

"He believes the world won't end this way. He thinks we will blow ourselves up long before a virus kills us."

"He really is mad. How long did you work for him?" Frank asked as they strolled over to the front door. Behind them the gate automatically closed.

"Too long."

When they reached the steel door, they heard the clunk of several locks being shifted, then the door creaked open. Standing before them was a man no bigger than a leprechaun. Okay, maybe that was an exaggeration. But he was a short little fucker. He was wearing a ruby red dressing gown, white muscle shirt, palm tree shorts, and bright yellow slippers. He squinted at them from behind small round spectacles on the end of his nose. In his hand was a .45 Magnum. It almost looked too large for him to hold.

"You crazy son of a bitch," Jameson said as he stepped forward. He only made it two steps when Abner cocked his gun.

"Money first."

"I should—"

"Really? You want to test me?" Abner growled.

"It's okay, Jameson." Frank thumbed off twenty-five hundred and went to give it to him but he instructed him to place it on the floor and then motioned with his gun for them to step back. They moved back about five feet.

"Keep going. Ten feet."

They backed up again. By now Jameson looked like he was going to blow his top. Abner pulled out a baggie and a pair of tweezers from his pocket. He approached the money and used the tweezers to pick up the notes and place them into the bag. All the while he kept his gun trained on them.

"Is that really necessary?" Jameson barked.

"Can't be too careful now with all these germs going around."

Frank smirked. He had gained a newfound respect for the guy. He wasn't doing anything Frank wouldn't have done.

"He has a point," Frank said.

Jameson rolled his eyes. Once Abner had stashed it away, he returned and motioned for them to go inside. They went in first and he followed. Frank noticed him give a nervous look around the yard before closing the vault-style door and then shifting home multiple locks on the other side.

"Quite a place you have here," Frank said.

"It does the job."

"I see you have cleaned up," Jameson said staring at the mess. Inside there were motor parts all over the place, a disassembled boat, and areas covered in grease. The smell of oil permeated the air as they stared at what he called home. It was more like a fortress. All the windows were barred and he had a room set up with surveillance that monitored at least twelve different areas at any given time.

"So, you're interested in guns? I hope you brought enough money. These babies are gold now."

"I'm sure we can reach a fair agreement," Frank muttered as they crossed a large living room. A TV was playing some old black-and-white comedy. Three shabby-looking cats looked up from their places on the furniture, one of them shot off and disappeared under a chair. The carpet on the ground had crumbs all over it. On the table was a bottle of whiskey and a smoldering cigar resting on the edge of an overloaded ashtray. It was clear the place hadn't seen a maid's touch in years.

As they followed him down a dimly lit corridor, they could hear some mumbling. Frank couldn't quite make out what it was but as they entered the kitchen area, his eyes widened. Strapped to a chair with no clothes on was a man who must have been in his late thirties. He was bound with a type of plastic that was usually seen wrapped around large pallets of boxes. His head hung down with a rag in his mouth, and his face was beaten to a pulp. It was hard to tell who he was without moving his head. There were battery cables attached to his nipples and the other ends hooked up to some electrical device.

Both Jameson and Frank stopped to take in the sight but Abner didn't even give the man a passing glance. He just kept pressing on to the next room as though he was going for a walk in the park.

Frank thumbed towards the guy and whispered to Jameson. "What the fuck?"

He shrugged. They caught up with the old guy who had already shuffled down the corridor and was calling for them to hurry up. They didn't dare ask him who the guy was. They had already experienced enough weird shit for one day.

"Come on. I don't have all day."

He brought them into what looked like a games room. There was a pool table, a dartboard on the wall, and a bar in the far corner. He went behind the carved mahogany bar and leaned down and brought up an unopened bottle of bourbon.

"Drink?"

They both nodded. It was hard to feel tough or superior to the old guy when they were standing in their underpants. Perhaps that's why he had done it. That or maybe he was just paranoid about people concealing weapons. He yanked the cap off and poured out three glasses, placed them on a tray, and brought them over to the pool table.

"Well, come and get."

He told them to stand at the far end of the table. That suited Frank fine. He was feeling a little anguish about being inside the guy's place. He made a mental note to take another pill when he got outside.

"A toast!"

"To what?"

"The end of the world."

"Not sure that's exactly something worth toasting to," Jameson muttered.

"It's exactly what this world needed. Hell, the place had already taken a nosedive. We have a shit president, a shit health care system, a military that abandons its vets, and a country full of self-entitled pricks."

All three of them held up their small shot glasses

before downing them. Frank tossed his over his shoulder. Who knew what was in it. He wasn't taking any chances.

"Two buttons. Don't ever press the one on the left," Abner said with a devilish grin. Frank had no idea what he was on about but Jameson must have as he was nodding.

Right then, Frank felt the ground beneath them shift. It sounded like a hydraulic system was moving. He turned to find that the floor they were standing on was lowering.

"What the…"

"Good, eh?" Abner grinned while pouring himself another drink. The entire pool table and floor around it went down about fifteen feet before stopping with a jolt. White fluorescent lights flashed on all around them. They were standing in a rectangular room. With all the walls covered in firearms of every type, it could have easily given the gun shop in town a run for its money. It had every kind of rifle, shotgun, handgun, and cowboy action weapon from the oldest to the newest.

"Isn't she a beauty?"

Frank looked on in bewilderment.

"I told you he had guns." Jameson's lip curled up.

# Chapter 9

Frank ran his fingers across the Uberti 1873 Sporting Rifle, then made his way down to the AK47s. It was a treasure trove of goodies.

"Where the hell did you get all these from?"

Abner gazed upon them like fine pieces of art. "You collect things, Frank?"

He thought about all the bottles of sanitizer he had stored at home. "Yeah, I guess so."

"It started out as a hobby, I would trade one gun in for another. Then I wanted to try out a variety and I guess I never kicked the habit. Some people collect guitars, some collect memorabilia, I collect guns."

"Are they all legal?" Frank asked him without even looking at him. He was mesmerized by all the options available to him.

Abner looked at Jameson, then back at Frank. "Does it matter now?"

Frank chuckled as he cast a glance at him. Abner looked like the midget version of Hugh Hefner, yet he gave off a degree of confidence that only came from having been in the military.

"Okay, let's get down to business. So how much do you want?" Frank asked.

"Two grand for any rifle, fifteen hundred for handguns."

Frank nearly choked. "Are you kidding me? That's daylight robbery."

"Supply and demand. Take it or leave it."

He had brought six grand with him. Twenty-five hundred he had already given to Abner. He had high hopes of getting a weapon for everyone on the island. If they were going to fend off attacks from the Guthries or anyone else that showed up, they were going to need some serious firepower, and ammo. A lot of ammo.

"And what about ammo?"

"Double what you would have paid down the gun shop."

"Come on, man, cut us a break."

"Look, if you are here to yank my chain, this concludes our business. You're lucky I'm even showing you this. If it wasn't for Jameson here, you would probably be hooked up to a chair like the fella upstairs."

Frank had his hand on an ARES-15 MCR Carbine. It was one hell of a gun. Just the kind of shit he needed to have at the house. He lifted his eyes to Abner. He couldn't resist asking.

"Who is he?"

"No clue but he jumped the fence and managed to break in through one of the back windows. I would have spotted him but I had a rough night."

"Still brewing that moonshine of yours, Abner?" Jameson started chuckling.

"I have a whole new batch. Stuff will knock you on your ass. I'd usually charge a hundred a bottle but I'm willing to do it for fifty."

"You are just full of deals, aren't you?" Frank said sarcastically.

"Not sure I like your tone."

"Well, you certainly know how to screw people over," Frank muttered.

"You want to say that again?"

It was almost comical coming from a man of his stature, Frank thought.

Jameson stepped in seeing that Abner was getting a little agitated. "He didn't mean anything by it, did you, Frank?"

Frank glared at him then looked away. "No, no I didn't."

"Yeah, cause you can go look elsewhere if you have a problem paying up."

"I have to arm around eight people and I have three and a half grand left for both weapons and ammo. What can you do for me?"

"I can show you the door." He spat a wad of tobacco from his mouth on the grated floor before chuckling. "Let me see. What do you like? Rifles, shotguns?"

"A long-distance rifle, a few semi-automatics, eight

handguns and enough ammo to last us for two months."

Abner shifted back from one foot to the next and looked at him. "Maybe you didn't hear me. I can sell you a weapon or two. This isn't a charity."

"Abner," Jameson said, trying to intervene.

"Don't Abner me. You still owe me twenty-five hundred."

"What? He just paid you."

"That was an admission fee," Abner shot back.

Jameson stepped forward and brought his finger up. "Are you kidding me, old man?"

Lightning fast, Abner grabbed his hand and twisted it around with all the speed of a gazelle. He locked his arm in place and Frank edged forward but was met by a tutting sound from his lips.

"I wouldn't advise it. I'll break his arm clean off and shove it up your ass. Now back up. Right now."

Jameson groaned, and winced as he started apologizing. Frank was beginning to see how the guy in the kitchen had got overpowered. Abner might not have looked like he packed much behind that flowing robe and thin shirt but he was no joke.

"Look, old man, just take it easy."

"I was killing gooks while your mothers were still wiping your asses. Now show me some damn respect."

Jameson got up and began rubbing his elbow. Frank placed on the table all the cash he had and pointed to different rifles and shotguns. "Just give me what you can for the money. The best you have, and maybe I'll come back tomorrow and buy some more."

A grin spread on Abner's face. He obviously relished pushing people around and making it clear that he wasn't a guy to be fucked with. They watched him load a black duffle bag with ammo, and stack up a couple of rifles and a handgun on the table along with several boxes of ammo.

"There, don't think I don't give out deals. That's more than anyone else would get."

As he zipped it up, an alarm went off and all the white lighting around them turned to red. It started flashing fast and Abner's eyes widened

"Motherfucker!" he hollered rushing over to the wall and smashing a red button. His robe swished in the air behind him like Superman's cape. The floor began rising.

"What the hell is going on?" Jameson asked.

"We've got a breach."

As the floor rose, he grabbed up the POF Renegade Generation 4 AR-15 off the table in front of him. He slapped in a magazine and got his jarhead face on.

"Those damn rats. I warned them. This time they are going to be spitting lead."

As soon as they were up, he was out of the room faster than they could take a few steps. For a guy with little legs he certainly could shift ass. They followed after him, taking a shotgun, and the P226 Sig Sauer he'd left on the table.

From down the corridor, they saw Abner shout at the bound man who had his head down. He drove the butt of his gun into the side of his temple and filled the air with cursing. As Frank passed by, he stopped and looked closely. He was out cold. Frank pulled up his head and stared for a second, then he realized who it was. It was Clarence, a cousin of Butch Guthrie. He'd seen him numerous times in Guthrie's store, helping out back. *Holy shit!* He dropped his head and raced after Jameson. By the time he reached the front of the house, Abner was unloading round after round outside. The noise was deafening until he stopped.

"Yeah, I warned you," Abner shouted.

"All we want is our cousin back."

"Well come and get him."

He chuckled and continued firing at them. He had this look of glee on his face as if he was reliving his years in the military. Frank envisioned him chasing after the Viet Cong through the jungles like an unleashed dog.

"Abner," Frank shouted but he couldn't hear him over the sound of rounds erupting. He wasn't just firing at them; they themselves were coming under fire from outside. He went over to a window and gazed out through makeshift blinds made of metal. When Abner was reloading, Frank caught a brief glimpse of Joey. *Was*

*Butch out there?*

"How many are there?" Frank asked.

"Two, I think," Jameson said. He had obviously spent far too much time around Abner as he was doing the same thing as him and unloading rounds.

Frank rushed over to Abner and grabbed him by the arm. "Abner, we should just let him go."

"Let him go? Are you out of your goddamn mind?"

"He's a Guthrie."

"And?"

Abner paid no attention; he pushed the muzzle of his gun back through a slat and peered through the scope. Frank went up to Jameson. "You need to get him to listen. These are not people to fuck with."

"Oh, but it's okay for you to?" Jameson replied.

Frank's brow knit together. "I had a plan. This isn't a plan. This is madness."

"This is survival," Abner shouted. "Now grow a pair and fire that weapon."

Frank rubbed his chin for a second. This wasn't the

way to deal with the situation. They might have been on the brink of seeing the country collapse but killing people? This fool was trigger-happy. He probably condoned it in his mind with some bull crap about how you would die first if you didn't shoot first. That was bullshit concocted from an ill mind of someone looking for a reason to kill.

"Abner! They just want their cousin."

"And I just want me some peace, but am I getting it? Hell no!" Abner continued his onslaught. There was no way he was going to be able to reason with him. Frank made his way back through the corridor down to the kitchen. He snatched a cooking knife off the counter and slashed away at Clarence's binds. He stared at him for a second from behind his mask and goggles and then threw caution to the wind. He hauled him up and swung an arm over his shoulder and was about to drag him out the back of the house when Abner came into the kitchen.

"What the hell do you think you're doing?"

"This is not right. There are ways to go about this.

Hand him over and they'll go away."

"Go away? Do you really think they are going to go away after what he's seen? Do you even know why I had him hooked up?"

"No but I'm sure you're going to give a good reason."

"I was interrogating him. Trying to find out why he was here."

"Perhaps he was looking for food."

"Really? Are you that naïve?" Abner shot back. He looked on edge. One minute he was looking at Frank, the next he was looking back down the corridor and shouting to Jameson to keep firing at them.

"I'm taking him out of here. You want to shoot me, go ahead."

The gun went off as Frank dragged Clarence towards the back door. It tore a hole in the wall. "The next one won't miss. Now put him down."

Frank hesitated for a moment and then he lowered him to the floor.

"Listen to me, Abner. I get it. I do. But holding him

here isn't going to make them go away. They know he's in here. Hell, they probably know we're in here. Now, until you bring him out and hand him over, they are going to keep trying to get in. Do you want that?"

Abner took a step back and regarded Frank with a confused look. "Have you even experienced war?"

Frank nodded. "I was a marine."

"Then you know that you don't just hand over the enemy."

"He's not the enemy."

Right then Jameson appeared in the doorway. "Your place was not the first to be hit by the Guthrie boys, Frank. They are going to keep doing it."

"Maybe so, but torturing a man in your kitchen is not the way to stop it."

"Really? What is?"

Frank didn't answer that.

Abner went over to a window and looked out and chuckled to himself. "Marine? You weren't a fucking marine. Any marine worth their salt knows there is a cost to war. We are not over there trying to win the hearts and minds of people. That's what politicians are for. The assholes in suits who would rather debate than pick up a gun."

"Fuck you, Abner."

Abner started back at him with a look of death. Abner pulled out his .45 Magnum from a holster around his waist and walked over to Frank. Frank didn't flinch as he brought it up to his face.

"You prepared to die, marine? Because I am, and so are they…"

Before Frank could do anything, Abner lowered the gun in one smooth motion and fired a round into Clarence's head. It blew the back of his head off and brain matter went all over the floor.

Startled, Frank stepped back.

"What the fuck. What the fuck!" Frank yelled.

"He wasn't going to tell me anything anyway."

With that said he turned to head out, leaving them there to look down at the bloody mess. Frank hadn't seen a dead body since his time in Iraq. It was a shock back then, and had been one of the many things that triggered his anxiety, and made him want to scrub himself clean.

Standing there, still holding the P226, he looked down and saw blood splatter all over his legs. Anxiety crept up fast into his chest and began to choke him. He had blood on him. He looked over to Jameson who was also standing there with nothing on except his boxers. What the hell were they thinking entering this madman's house?

"Frank. Frank!" Jameson tried to snap him out of the trance-like state he was in. His hand trembled. Whatever PTSD he'd suffered from war came back with a fury. Whatever repulsion he had to germs was now at the forefront of his mind. All he could see was blood all over the place and germs seeping into the cells of his body. He moved quickly over to the sink and turned the faucet on. He washed the blood from his legs, leaving a puddle of water on the tiled floor, and reached for a dirty tea towel to dry off. His skin was crawling and he found himself hyperventilating.

"We need to get out of here," Frank muttered.

The sound of gunfire continued as Abner unleashed a flurry of rounds and hollered at the Guthries like an insane patient who was off his meds. They heard the door unlock and Abner stepping outside.

"Come on, you fuckers! You want some. Come and get it."

The snap of bullets ricocheting off metal rattled Frank's nerves.

Abner was completely out of his mind. Not thinking about the danger involved or if he would get caught in the act, Frank moved down the corridor fast and entered the room they had been in. He went back over to the pool table and felt around for the button on the right, beneath the table, that Abner had pressed. The system kicked in and began lowering. Jameson entered and asked him what he was doing. He didn't reply.

As soon as it reached the next floor he started filling the long black duffel bag with more guns. He added several AR-15's, a sniper rifle, and as many handguns as he could jam into the bag along with boxes of ammo. By the time he zipped that up, he had to use both hands to haul it up onto the table. He slapped the red button and exhaled hard as the contraption began to rise up again.

Once it was back up, Jameson was still there standing at the doorway looking fearful.

"Give me a hand, we are getting the fuck out of here."

Jameson rushed in and grabbed a handle while Frank had the other and they hauled it out of the room and towards the back door. They hadn't even reached it before they heard Abner's voice.

"Going somewhere?"

# Chapter 10

Abner had stepped over a line. As much as Frank needed the guns and had a plan in mind of how to retrieve what Butch had taken, he hadn't though about those in town who would shoot first and ask questions later. Perhaps, in the time that he had lived with Kate, her softhearted nature had worn away at his stony exterior? Or maybe he wasn't ready to accept that the country had reached the point of killing each other to survive.

"Now hold on, Abner," Jameson said setting the bag down and raising a hand. "We just want to get out of here and get back to the island."

"What have you got in the bag?"

"Just a few more rifles. I'll be back to pay you for the rest."

His nostrils flared. "The hell you will."

There was at least thirty yards between them, the sound of gunfire was still occurring outside but Abner was no longer concerned about them, he just wanted to make damn sure that Frank didn't walk off with his merchandise.

"Abner, you have more than enough down there. I've left the three and a half thousand, I'll be back for the rest."

"Well when you do, then you can take the guns. Until then they stay here."

As he began walking towards them, he stepped into a ray of light seeping in from outside. Whether it was coming from one of the many windows, or bullet holes in the walls, they couldn't tell. He hadn't made it but a few feet when more gunfire erupted and Abner reached up to the side of his neck. He began wobbling ever so slightly as he brought his hand out and looked at the blood. It had hit an artery as blood was firing out the side of his throat. Within seconds he crumpled to the floor and his gun went off as he landed.

"Let's go," Frank said hauling the bag up.

Jameson stood there staring at his body.

"Jameson, come on."

He yanked at his arm and he snapped out of it. They rushed out of the back of the home and came around the side. Dropping the bag on the ground, they both took out an AR-15 and slammed a magazine in each. Crouched down at the corner of the house, Frank peered around the side towards the main gate. It was still closed. Joey and three other men had climbed over and were positioned in various places around the lot. Some of them had ducked down at the corners of cars and were continuing to take potshots at the house.

"Do you know another way out of here?"

"Well, yeah, we can head over the fence and make our way along the shoreline but we're liable to break our neck on the rocks, long before we make it around."

Their clothes, and the truck they'd arrived in were still outside the gate. The odds of being able to fend them off or drive away were slim to none, unless they were prepared to kill or be killed. Right now his mind was still reeling from watching an innocent man get a bullet in the head.

"They aren't going to stop until they get inside," Frank muttered.

"Did you lock the pool table?"

"Does it matter?" Frank said before returning to looking at what Joey was telling one of his men. He watched them shift position. Each time they did the others would cover for the one moving.

Jameson grabbed his arm. "No, you don't understand. You have to press the button twice to get it to lock in place. If it doesn't, the moment someone steps on the outer perimeter, it will go back down. It has a sensor built into the panels around the floor."

"Who cares, let them have it," Frank said turning back towards the cars.

Jameson wouldn't let up. "Listen, we are going to need more than what we have here. You want all that firepower to end up in their hands?"

Frank exhaled hard. He gave another look around the corner and then started moving back. "Alright, stay here,

I'll go back in."

Frank moved around him and darted back inside. Though he knew Abner was dead he couldn't help feel as if his ghost was lurking over his shoulder and telling him to stay away from his property. Stupid old coot. If he hadn't held on to that Guthrie, they would have left. Frank darted into the room and rushed over to the table.

When Jameson had created it, he'd been smart enough to make the buttons look like just another section of the table. Frank fumbled around underneath until his fingers found the buttons. His finger touched the one on the left and he wondered what it did. Maybe it was curiosity, the leftovers of a child's need to rebel, but he couldn't resist. He pressed the left button for just a few seconds and flames shot out the sides. Holy crap! After releasing, he pressed the right one to lock the table in place and was about to leave the room when he heard voices inside.

They had made their way in.

"He's over here, Joey," one of the others in the group said.

Frank backed up from the corridor.

"Oh, God. Fuck!" Joey hollered. Frank's immediate thought was they had found Clarence.

Frank pressed his shoulder into the wall and peered around, looking down the corridor. One way he saw Joey and several others, the other way he saw Jameson. He briefly poked his head around the door, no doubt coming to warn him. A little late for that now. Frank motioned to Jameson to get the hell out.

"Go check the rooms. Clarence believed this asshole had weapons."

"Where?" Dusty said.

"How the hell should I know? Clarence was the only one who knew about it. Take Palmer and Jackson." They turned and started heading down the hall. There were four rooms in that corridor. The room Frank was inside was the last one on the right. One against three, he didn't like those odds. He turned and looked around for a place to hide. Besides the pool table and the bar, there was nowhere else, except...

He looked up and saw panels that could be pushed up. "Ah fuck this," Frank said. He brought up his rifle, and stood beside the door waiting for one of them to enter. His body trembled.

Seconds felt like minutes as he heard boots getting closer. He pressed himself hard against the wall with the rifle raised. The very second the guy stepped foot inside the room, Frank jammed the butt of his gun hard into his temple. He was out cold before he even hit the floor. Not wasting another second, he rushed out holding his weapon high expecting to run into one of them but they had gone into individual rooms. The only one that spotted him was Joey, who was still in the kitchen.

Frank unloaded several rounds, purposely making sure to miss but scare him enough that he would dive for cover. All the while he rushed backwards towards the exit. As soon as he broke out into the warm summer air, he double-timed around the building heading for the fence.

Jameson was already over and had started the truck. He could hear yelling behind him as Joey and his men scrambled to come after him. Frank vaulted over that fence with all the finesse of an Olympic gymnast. As gunfire erupted behind him, he landed hard on the other side. He certainly wasn't scoring a gold for that landing. He tripped and nearly fell on his face as he rushed to get up and scoop up his pile of clothes. But they were already gone. He figured Jameson had taken them. Jameson was already backing up as he sprinted towards the truck. He lunged for the back and threw himself over into the bed as Jameson sped away under a hail of bullets.

Slamming around in the back of the truck, he tried to get up but Jameson wasn't easing off the gas. He was only going faster. Every bump and hole in the road made him slam against the side, or gain air. Several times he thought he was going to come out of the back of that truck. How he managed to stay inside was beyond him.

The truck burst out of Cottage Road and took a sharp right, slamming him into the side again. This time he felt a shot of pain go through his shoulder. The exhaust pipe let out a guttural cry as the 4 x 4 Ford truck accelerated forward leaving behind a plume of dust.

When Frank managed to get to the window he noticed that Jameson was still not back in his clothes. The bag with the firearms was on the seat.

"Where are my clothes?"

"How the hell should I know? I didn't see them on the ground, I figured they must have grabbed them up."

"You want to slow down before I end up as roadkill?"

Jameson's eyes swept the mirrors like a psychotic mental patient. Frank was just about to tell him to ease off the gas again because no one was following when the passenger side mirror exploded and several rounds hit the back of the truck. He twisted to see a black truck bursting through a dusty landscape.

"You've got to be kidding!"

He slipped down, trying to stay low while at the same time lifting his rifle and returning fire. He didn't dare lift his head up and he had no idea if any of the rounds were hitting the vehicle behind them.

Bullets snapped over his head, one struck the back

window on the truck and in the next second he found himself covered in tiny shards of glass.

"Motherfuckers!" Jameson yelled.

They were on NY-12 heading west towards Clayton. The road was desolate, the landscape flat and there were minimal homes along the way. It was pretty much farmland. They shot past a sign on the right-hand side for some beauty shop.

He could hear the roar of the truck's engine behind as it was gaining on them.

"You want to keep firing at them?" Jameson yelled. It was a surreal moment for sure. Frank felt like he was having an out-of-body experience in which he was looking down on himself, wearing nothing but a pair of underpants, a face mask, goggles, and boots. He lifted the rifle again and unleashed another flurry of bullets, this time he moved in a sweeping motion.

"Beauty!" Jameson screamed out loud. His cry was followed by a crunch of metal and a thud. Frank raised himself up on his elbows and looked over the rim of the truck bed. In a cloud of dust and dirt was the truck that had been pursuing them. It had come off the road into a farmer's field. Smoke was pouring out of the engine, the windscreen was cracked and the occupants were pushing their way out.

Frank gazed back down the road behind them and breathed a sigh of relief. There were no more vehicles chasing after them. Jameson was hooting and hollering about what an adrenaline rush that was. Adrenaline? Frank could have done without being shot at.

As they bumped their way down to Jameson's house, Frank cleared glass off his chest. In a few areas he was cut but it wasn't too bad. When Jameson killed the engine, he hopped out and looked at the sorry state Frank was in.

"What a ride, eh?"

He groaned, reaching for his lower back. "I'm gonna feel this tomorrow."

"Need a hand?"

Frank grabbed hold of his and clambered over the side onto the ground. Jameson burst out laughing. "Ah man, you should get a load of us. What has this world come to?"

That's when Frank noticed that Jameson was bleeding.

"Your shoulder."

"Ah," he shrugged. "Don't worry about it. It's just a graze."

As they made their way down to the dock and back into the boat, Frank glanced around at the neighbors' homes. A week ago, neighbors might have called police, and had them locked up for indecent exposure, or men in white coats might have taken them away and tossed them in a padded cell.

One thing was for sure. They weren't in Kansas anymore. No police were coming to protect or arrest them. No one was coming to give Clarence or the psychotic Abner Rooney a proper burial. They would go the way that others would in this new world. They would be left to rot and their carcasses would eventually be eaten away by insects and small animals that would make their way inside.

Once they tossed the bag of guns in the boat, Jameson took Frank inside his home and gave him a shirt, and a pair of his old pants. They were tight as Jameson had a small frame but at least it would save him the ridicule he would have got had he returned without any pants.

Inside the home as Jameson got ready, Frank walked around the quiet living room. There were a few pieces of furniture, a cabinet full of crystal, and several photos of Jameson, Meg, and his stepdaughter. An upright piano was off to his right. He lifted the lid and ran his hand across the keys. It let out an out-of-tune sound and he lowered it. On a side table he saw a bottle of bourbon. He scooped it up, unscrewed the top, and gave it a sniff. He wasn't a big drinker but that smelled damn good. Frank opted to not have any and instead picked up the photo. He heard the floorboards creak behind him and he looked around to find Jameson doing up the buttons on his shirt.

"That's Meg, and Kiera in better days."

"Where is she now? I mean, did you bury her?"

"No. Doctors wouldn't let me in to see her. They told

me she had passed and because of how infectious the virus was, I wasn't able to see her."

"That sucks. Probably for the best though," Frank said placing the frame back down. "We should probably get going."

"Do you think this is it?"

Frank frowned. "What?"

"The end?"

He shrugged. "My wife was pretty certain that they aren't going to be able to reel this one in."

"Where is she?"

"Atlanta. She works for the CDC." He ran a hand around the back of his neck to work out some of the tension.

"Alive?"

"As far as I know. I haven't heard from her in several days so I'm not sure if she will try to make her way here. She was about to get married to someone else. He's dead now."

Jameson leaned against the frame of the French doors

that separated the living room from the kitchen. "I've never given much thought to how I would die. You know, I guess it's one of those things you tend to put off thinking about until you're faced with some health crisis. Now it feels like I'm staring down the barrel of a gun. One part of me just wants to join Meg and the other keeps telling me to stick around for Kiera's sake."

Frank nodded. "That's a good reason."

"You ever thought of… you know…"

Frank chuckled. "Trust me. I've been there countless times and it didn't take a pandemic to get me there. It's not a good place to be in," Frank said before heading towards the back door.

Jameson asked one last question, "So how did you overcome that?"

Frank placed his hand on the knob of the door and opened it. He didn't look at him when he answered. "I didn't. I just take it one day at a time."

# Chapter 11

Back on the island, Ella was in the middle of planting potatoes in a small plot out the back of the cottage. She had taken several of the potatoes that Jameson had brought over prior to leaving and had sliced them into several parts. They key was not to plant the entire potato but to locate the eyes of the potato and cut it in half or in three pieces depending on where the growing points were. She was just about to bury them when someone blocked out the sun.

"Aren't you supposed to leave them in a pantry for a day or two to heal over before you plant them?"

She snorted. "Gardener, are we?" she said, looking up and seeing Gabriel there.

He crouched down and assessed her handiwork. "My grandfather was. When I was little he would take us out back and get us involved in planting different seeds and helping out around the garden. He loved that plot."

"Is he still alive?"

"Oh no, he passed away a good seven years ago, not long after my grandmother."

"Sorry to hear that."

He shrugged. It didn't seem to bother him much. Time had a way of doing that.

"I'll give you a hand."

"Aren't you meant to be keeping a watch out for the Guthries?"

He nodded. "That's right but I don't think we are going to come under attack, do you?"

She pushed a piece of potato down into the earth. Each one would be around twelve inches apart and three inches below soil. They had to be placed in an area that got at least six hours of sun a day.

"You've always lived in the big city, haven't you?"

"What makes you say that?"

"Just a guess. Am I right?"

His lip curled up. "You are. And?"

"City folk tend to spend so much time looking up at the

skyscrapers and avoiding eye contact, they can overlook the ones in front of them."

"What does that mean?"

"It means it can be a good and a bad thing."

He scoffed and handed her another potato to plant. "Ella Talbot, you don't make much sense."

"Hey! Where's my water?" Tyrell's voice carried on the wind from across the tiny island.

"Yeah, yeah, it's coming." He rose up and looked down at her. "I'll speak to you later."

She nodded but didn't reply. As he walked away she cupped a hand over her eyes and watched him hurry into the house. After she had filled the trench, and covered it over, she went into the shed and retrieved the binoculars. She came out and wandered down to the water's edge to see if she could see her father returning. She focused in on an area of water between their island and the mainland and it took her a few minutes before she saw the boat returning, and her father inside. She turned and let her gaze drift across the water to the other islands. There was another one close by called Watch Island. It was partially attached by way of a small series of rocks. She couldn't see any movement over there. It was privately owned and the last thing she had heard was that the current owners were trying to sell it for close to two million dollars.

She continued looking around until she noticed a group of people standing on the dock of Club Island, which was a section of Grindstone Island. She zoomed in to get a better look and that's when she realized one of them was looking back at her through a set of binoculars. It was Butch Guthrie.

Moving fast up the embankment, she disappeared into the thick tree line that surrounded the property and made a dash for the house. When she burst into the kitchen through the rear door, she startled Gloria and Sal who were in the middle of what appeared to be a heated conversation.

"He knows we're here," she said out of breath while steadying herself against the kitchen counter.

"What?" Sal replied.

"Butch Guthrie. I just saw them looking this way."

Sal looked as if he was about to have a coronary, he raced outside the house with Gloria not far behind him.

"Sal. Wait up."

"That bastard is going to pay."

Gabriel had been getting a couple of bottles of water from the basement when Ella headed out after Sal.

"Sal, my father is on his way back. There's nothing you can do without a ride."

The only boat they had belonged to Jameson and it was on its way back.

"I'll swim."

"Don't be stupid," Gloria hollered.

"What's going on?" Gabriel yelled as he joined the rest of them. Ella brought him up to speed but Sal was already down by the water taking off his clothes.

"Sal, you're not thinking straight," Ella said rushing down to where he was while trying to divert her eyes away from the sight of his piss-stained briefs. "Just wait until my father gets back. Heck, you were the one telling him not to be hasty."

"That was then, this is now."

She shook her head in desperation.

Seeing that he wasn't listening to her, she looked to Gabriel and Tyrell who were just watching with a look of amusement. What on earth they found funny about this situation was unknown but then again seeing a psychiatrist testing the water with his toes to see how cold it was before he made a brave attempt to cross was kind of funny.

"Well, are you two just going to stand there?" she said.

They rushed down the embankment and grabbed a hold of him and began hauling him back.

"Get off."

"Sorry, no can do."

Ella knew full well he wasn't going to get in that water the moment he touched it. Even though it was the middle of summer it was freezing cold. And the distance between the two islands was too far for someone to swim. He was just putting on a front for Gloria who was eating it up.

This was probably the first time she had ever seen him standing up for her.

Eventually they managed to talk him down from the ledge so to speak. Gloria had run in to get him a towel, even though he didn't need one. Ella rolled her eyes and made her way back to the house. By the time they had got him inside, her father came through the front door. He stood there for a second gazing at them all gathered around Sal who was sitting on a chair in his underwear.

"Let me guess, you took a trip to see Abner as well," he muttered with a grin.

"What?"

No one had a clue about what he was on about until later that evening when he filled them in on what had happened. It was strange to see people go from roaring with laughter to deadpan serious in a matter of seconds when he and Jameson told them about the attack.

One thing was clear, they had just opened a can of worms and all hell was going to break loose.

\* \* \*

"I'm telling you, we have to do this tonight. He knows we're here," Frank said.

"Okay, let's say you succeed. You now have the food back, then what? You think he is going to stand by and do nothing?" Zach said.

"No. But do you want to starve?"

"We can rotate shifts. The fact that we are on an island and there is some distance between us and them means we don't need a fence to keep them out, the water is our fence," Ella said. "The island's not big so if three or four us stay awake at night and then sleep in the day, we should be able to keep them away."

"Right, I can see that working — not!" Hayley said shifting from one foot to the other. She and Ella exchanged an icy glare.

"Listen. I'm not saying this is going to be easy but we have few options. Now I'm more than willing for us to go scouting around in the town but the same amount of danger exists there as it does going over to Grindstone and getting my stuff," Frank said.

"How so?" Tyrell asked.

"Abner is a prime example. The guy was holed up in his house and he fired before we even spoke with him. People are on edge. They are going to defend what they have, if they have anything at all. After seeing Joey and the others in town, I wouldn't be surprised if Butch and his mob have already begun making their way through homes."

There was an awkward silence between them all.

"You mentioned that they don't know us. What about if we head over there like you said? Feel the place out. Find out where they've got the food stored and see how many are there," Gabriel chimed in.

"No, you can't do that," Hayley said.

"What else do you want us to do?" he asked, turning to her. She shook her head and walked out of the room.

"Look, chances are, Butch isn't in a hurry to head over here immediately. They already got what they needed from here. It's a risky move to do it again. Especially when they don't know who's on the island."

No one seemed to be in agreement. There was a lot of

back and forth but Frank knew that without knowing what they were up against, they couldn't exactly storm in there with guns blazing. It was the reason why Butch had visited prior to Frank leaving for Queens. It wasn't just a neighborly visit. He was spying. Getting a feel for what he was up against. They were going to need to do the same thing.

Sal got up and began changing back into his clothes. Gloria went and put on a pot of tea and Zach and Tyrell returned to keeping an eye on the water, taking with them an AR-15 each. Frank told them he would be out there soon to take them through how to use one. They nodded and wandered off. Gabriel was about to go with them when Frank asked to have a word with him.

He looked back over his shoulder. "Yeah, sure. What's up?"

Frank motioned towards his study on the far side of the house. He led him through one of the corridors and they entered. It wasn't big, just enough room for a table and a few shelves with books. He kept some of the classics, and some old encyclopedias on medicine and disease. Kate's fascination with disease had led him into research. He missed having her around. Bouncing ideas off her and just feeling her warm body in bed with him at night.

Gabriel took a seat across from him.

Frank studied him and leaned back in his chair. "You know you don't have to do this."

"I know. But its the least I can do."

"You understand that you won't be able to go in there with any weapons, right?"

He nodded. "I understand."

"And we're going to need to find another boat. After hearing Sal whine and moan about how cold the water is, I would feel bad asking you to swim."

When Gabriel didn't reply, he kind of figured that wasn't something he wanted to do. It was more of a last resort idea if they couldn't find another boat. There had to be more out there. Not everyone would have resorted to stealing boats.

"You ever fired a gun, Gabriel?"

"I've been at a firing range before. My old man used to go."

"And Tyrell and Zach?"

"Well, I'm thinking it might be better to leave them here, you know, to keep watch over this place. Besides, if anything goes wrong, I would hate to have all of us caught up in it."

"I'll go with him," a voice said from behind them. The door was slightly ajar and Ella was standing there.

"You're not going," Frank immediately replied.

Ella leaned against the doorframe. "I'm not a kid anymore."

"It doesn't matter."

"What, so my life is more important than his?"

Frank frowned. "I didn't mean that." He looked at Gabriel. "Really, I didn't mean that."

"No? Then why not?"

"Because he knows you, Ella. He's seen you before. This can only work if he's approached by people he doesn't know."

"And you think he's just going to open his arms and let Gabriel walk into the midst of them?"

Frank rubbed both hands over his face and then rested his elbows on the table while he kneaded the bridge of his nose with two fingers.

"There are a lot of variables at work here. I'm going with the ones that…" he trailed off. There was no way to cherry coat it. It was dangerous sending anyone in there. In many ways, it was no different than walking up to a house in the town and asking to be let in. Gabriel was liable to get beaten, and even shot if Frank was being honest. Then again, he was sure that Gabriel was aware of the danger otherwise he wouldn't have volunteered or agreed to the half-baked plan.

"Then what?"

"Ella, just…"

"If she's going, so am I." The competitive voice of Hayley chimed in from behind Ella. Frank placed a hand on his forehead. *Oh great. This is all I need.*

"Look, if I had my way none of you would be going. And

I would do it myself but that's not happening."

Gabriel turned in the swivel chair. "He's right. It's too dangerous for you both to go in."

Ella placed a hand on her hip. "What, because we're women?"

"I didn't say that," Gabriel replied.

"But you were implying it," Hayley took the same stance as Ella.

First they were at each other's throats, now they were standing together over a seemingly innocent response.

"Well hey, you want to get shot, raped, or killed then be my guest," Gabriel said spinning back around in the leather chair.

That wasn't exactly instilling confidence in Frank. He hadn't gone through hell and back to get his daughter only to lose her. That wasn't going to happen.

Right then, Gloria came in with a tray of tea and placed it on the table. Frank couldn't believe he was having this conversation. It seemed too surreal. Only a week ago, he was thinking it would be only Ella, Sal, and him on the island and now they had a whole group full of more issues than he was prepared to deal with. He couldn't believe that Gloria was serving tea in his house as though nothing was happening. And yet he knew it was her way of dealing with the unrest. No one truly knew the best way to go about dealing with the present. But one thing was sure, it had come down to a matter of survival. Butch knew that. That's why he had waltzed in there and robbed them blind. He was hedging his bets, stocking his storehouse in preparation for the winter, and it was going to be one hell of a winter. But that was months from now. They had to deal with what was before them and right now that meant finding out more about the enemy.

# Chapter 12

Butch kicked a pail of water across the grass before grabbing hold of Joey by the ear and yelling at the others. Contrary to how people viewed him, he didn't like getting angry for no reason. If he was honest, he actually felt bad about it but he didn't ever tell them that. He couldn't because they feared him. That kind of respect couldn't be bought. It was earned.

"I send you to do one damn thing and you couldn't even do that? Not only do you return empty-handed but you tell me my cousin is dead?"

"I'm sorry, Butch, we were outnumbered. There had to have been at least twenty of them."

"Twenty?"

Joey nodded while wincing and bending at the waist.

"Was it twenty, Dusty?"

Dusty cleared his throat and looked at Joey as if he was considering his answer. "There was a lot. More than we could deal with. We're lucky we got out of there with our own lives."

Butch released his vise-like grip on Joey and paced back and forth. "Why do I get the feeling you aren't telling me the truth?"

He looked upon them cowering before him and a warm sense of satisfaction came over him. It didn't matter that they had screwed up, only that they continued to show him the respect he deserved.

"And who was leading this group?"

They were hesitant to reply but Jackson spoke up, "It was Frank Talbot."

Butch stopped in his tracks. "Talbot?"

It was getting late in the day and the sun was beginning to wane behind the trees. He hadn't been able to get a good look at who was on Talbot's island because of all the trees shrouding his view but he was pretty damn sure that Gloria wasn't alone anymore. But twenty people? Could he really have gathered that many together? Had that been the reason he had left? He ran a hand over his face. Now that could be a problem, he thought. His mind was bombarded by paranoia. Was he seeking retribution? If so, why had he gone to the mainland? Twenty people? He couldn't wrap his head around that. He'd been thinking of paying a visit to his island that evening but after this, no, he had to rethink this through. If they had shot Clarence, execution style, what would they do to him? He had a large family and plenty of firearms but even with all his brothers, sisters, and cousins those were some tough odds. Unless…

"Ring the bell, and get the family together. We are going to have a meeting later this evening. Tell everyone, including the families that chose to remain on the island, to get over to Dodge Hall once it's dark."

"And what if they don't want to come?" Joey asked

Butch rushed over to him and grabbed him by the ear again. "Then make them. Grow a pair and start showing me you can actually step up to the plate and do something right."

"You got it, Butch." He cowered away with the others

and they broke into a sprint, heading towards to the ATV's. As the engines roared to life and he watched them leave to alert the others, it was pleasing to the eye, if only to give him a false sense of control.

* * *

After debating the best course of action, it was decided that Gabriel and Tyrell would go over to the island. Ella fought Frank on the decision, and Hayley didn't look thrilled, but the decision was final.

Frank would take them across to the mainland and once they found a boat, they would head over and tell Butch they were from Watertown and were trying to escape the virus that was spreading across the country.

They would stay there for forty-eight to seventy-two hours or until they could determine what Butch was up to and where he was keeping his supplies.

"So run this by me again, we are basically like a Trojan horse?" Tyrell said.

"Something like that," Gabriel replied.

"Great, I feel like a lamb being led to the slaughter."

Frank was heading east on NY-12 in Jameson's pickup truck, towards Clayton Distillery. Before leaving the island, Jameson had told him that he knew a guy over on Washington Island, a small island connected to the village by way of the causeway. He was adamant that the guy wouldn't have left his property and would be more than accommodating to lend them his boat in exchange for some alcohol.

"Are you sure?"

"Yeah, he's a raging drunk. I guarantee it. Make sure it's the two-dog moonshine. The old coot is crazy about that stuff."

"Please tell me I'm not going to have to take my clothes off again, am I?"

Jameson let out a laugh and patted him on the back before they left.

Now, as they made their way to the distillery, Frank couldn't help wonder if the guy was going to be a raving lunatic like Abner Rooney. At least now, all three of them were armed.

A deep orange sky stretched out before them as they made it to the other side.

"I don't see why we couldn't just take Jameson's boat."

"Because we might need it, besides if Butch catches wind that we were on the island without a boat, he's going to put two and two together."

"By the sound of what Sal was saying, this Butch can barely spell, never mind count," Tyrell muttered.

Frank snorted. Butch might have acted as dumb as a mule in the past but he wasn't going to lower his guard. Frank never underestimated anyone. In Iraq it could get you killed. He'd seen friends of his approach women that were all smiles only to get blown apart when it was discovered they were wearing a suicide vest. Years in the military had taught him to trust no one, except his brothers in arms. As the truck bumped its way down the road, he thought back to those days. Things were different back then, though he struggled with anxiety, and fought hard to hide his fear of germs, they were some of the better days of his life.

There was something very primal about being stuck in the middle of a dust-filled village kicking in doors, hearing thousands of people chanting their prayers at night in the distance, never knowing when and where they would try to attack.

It made him appreciate the quiet moments. The down time, even the conversations he had with fellow soldiers when they got assigned to shit-burning duty. He winced, at the thought. He could still smell it.

"So, Ella told us you were in the military."

"I was."

"So what was that like?"

He cast a glance over to them. Two young guys, just at the beginning of their lives, had no idea. No words could explain it, or at least sum it up. There was no palatable sound bite, people had to go and see for themselves. He hadn't stayed in contact with anyone from the military since leaving. After getting back he just wanted to be left alone. Nothing that he did over there felt special, and yet like other jarheads, he didn't want civilians to forget.

He was about to answer but they were getting close to the distillery.

"Are you sure the cops aren't still active?"

"Believe me, they are long gone."

He veered right in front of the River Golf sign and down onto the gravel driveway that led up to the one-story shack. Made from knotty pine planks, it stood out like a sore thumb against the backdrop of fields. The place had always reminded Frank of an old church without a steeple. The lot was empty and from the looks of it the neighboring mini golf establishment was the same. The fear of that which could kill preceded any need to earn a living. How long it would remain like that was unknown but he was pretty sure their doors wouldn't open again.

"Right, listen up, once inside we find the moonshine and get the hell out. I don't want to be dicking around here."

"Why would we?" Gabriel asked. Frank looked past him to Tyrell. It wasn't Gabriel he was concerned about.

The entire journey back from Queens had been like a nonstop joke to this kid. It was only when they arrived in Watertown and he discovered his parents were dead, that the other shoe dropped. For a while Frank thought that might be the turning point for him but nope, it didn't take him long to return to acting like a jackass.

"Just, stay close."

Frank hopped out and pulled out his rifle from the back of the truck and double-timed it around the rear of the building. He used the butt of his gun to break a window. As the glass shattered on the floor inside, he waited for an alarm to go off but there was nothing.

"Looks like you were worrying about a whole load of nothing, Mr. T."

"I told you to stop calling me that."

"Take a chill pill, old man."

Tyrell scoffed as he made his way inside. He used his jacket to cover the frame of the window and with the assistance of both of them he clambered in. Next was Gabriel then Frank. Once in, all three of them took in the sight of the rectangular loft-style building. At one end was a store where they sold shirts, hats, and alcohol and at the other end was a distillery filled with large metal vats.

Tyrell was in the middle of saying how easy it was to get inside when Frank spotted the sensor in the far corner. Before he could grab Tyrell, he stepped right into its line of sight. Alarm bells started ringing. It was deafening.

"Find the panel to turn that shit off."

Frank rushed to one end while the others went to the other and scrambled around looking for an alarm system. A few minutes into the ear-bleeding noise, it stopped. He exhaled and turned to see Tyrell holding several wires in his hand.

"Found it."

Over the next five minutes they searched the store and filled up a bag with four bottles of moonshine. They had three different flavors: lemonade, cherry, and apple. As Frank filled up a bag, Tyrell gasped as if he had just chugged down some. Sure enough, when he turned he was holding a bottle with the cap off and staring down at it.

"50.5 percent proof. Damn, this stuff is delicious."

Frank charged over and yanked it out of his hand. He immediately began protesting.

"Hey, what's up your ass?" Tyrell said.

"I need you to stay sober."

He scoffed and then grabbed up another bottle and unscrewed it in front of him like an unruly child.

"Seriously?"

"Well, I hear a lot about what you need, but what about what I need? Or Gabriel needs? Huh?"

"Tyrell, just put it down," Gabriel said.

"Oh, what so you are on his side now?"

"This isn't about sides, dude. He's right, we need to stay clear-headed if we are going to pull this off."

Tyrell pulled both arms out and bowed a little as if mocking Frank. "Well excuse me, the lord almighty has spoken. I forgot that we are the ones putting our neck on the line."

Frank shook his head. He really was in no mood for

his shit. "You agreed."

"That's right I did, and the way I see it, if I'm liable to get killed going over there then I should at least enjoy myself before I go." He gazed at all the bottles of alcohol lining the shelves. "I mean, just look at this. Haven't you ever wanted to do this? You know, break into a place and get absolutely shit-faced?"

Frank shook his head and strolled off. "Gabriel, you want to speak some sense into him before I use another method."

"Another method? What are you gonna do? Huh?"

Gabriel stepped forward as Tyrell took another swig from the bottle.

"Come on, man, just put it down and let's go."

"No. Screw that. I haven't had a minute to stop and think since Watertown. It's all been about getting Ella back, and finding a boat, and getting revenge on some asshole, who I couldn't give two shits about." He paused and looked at them, his features hardened. "What about what I want? What about what I *need?*"

"Look, there will be plenty of time to reflect after."

Frank stood by the door watching Gabriel try to negotiate with his friend. As much as he didn't have time for this, he hadn't stopped to think about how the loss of Tyrell's parents might have affected him. There were no tears when he came out of his home in Watertown. No sense that it had bothered him beyond a shrug or a distant glance. But it had. How could it not? Of course, he'd been driven to get Ella to safety and without their supplies they weren't going to last long. But, Tyrell was right, the train they were on just kept chugging, and slowing down or jumping off just wasn't in the cards. The moment that virus breached those barricades, the moment it killed the first human being, life as they knew it changed. It was a hard reality to get used to and one that none of them were comfortable with.

"Well maybe I should just stay here. I mean we're all eventually going to die, aren't we? It's only a matter of time." Tyrell strolled over to some bottles and ran his hand across them.

"So what? You're going to drink yourself to death," Gabriel said walking over to him.

"Maybe."

"Why then did you even agree to come?" Gabriel asked. "Zach would have taken your place. We need to do this now."

"There you go again with what you need. I don't hear me, in any of that."

"Because this isn't just about you, Tyrell. It's about Gabriel, Zach, Hayley, Ella, Sal and his family. I know you're hurting right now but this is not the time," Frank said.

"Really? When is the time? Because the way I see it, we are running out of time. All we have is now. None of us know if we are going to be alive tomorrow."

"How was that any different before the pandemic?" Gabriel said.

"What do you mean?"

"I mean, when it's your time, it's your time."

He shook his head and pursed his lips. "It's not the

same."

"No? My old man thought he would get more years than he did. You saw him before he died. He was a shell of a man. The fact is, the only thing you have said that makes sense, is that all we have is now... so we need to make the most of it. And I for one, am not going to die in some distillery from alcohol poisoning."

Tyrell stared blankly at him and then took one more swig before he tossed the bottle across the room and it shattered into pieces on the ground. He passed by Frank and scowled at him.

"Happy now?" Tyrell said before opening the door.

A voice bellowed from beyond the doors. "Police! Don't move!"

## Chapter 13

Sal stood at the top of the ladder hammering in another sign. He had put up four so far. The idea had come to him while he was rooting around in Frank's shed.

"You really think that's going to work?" Ella said cupping a hand over her eyes as she looked up.

"For the Guthries, no, but for others I think it's a deterrent. It might make them think twice about boarding the island."

"They won't see it at night."

He paused with a nail in his hand. "Right, I didn't think about that. Has he got any luminous paint?"

"No."

He groaned. "Well, it will have to do."

In large letters of blue paint, he had created foreboding signs that said *BIOHAZARD: There are infected people on this island* and *QUARANTINE: Some inhabitants of this island are infected.*

He had one posted at the boat dock, and others nailed into trees on either side of the island. While Frank was on the mainland he had to do something, anything to keep his mind occupied. Everything inside of him wanted to head over to Grindstone and end the pitiful life of Butch Guthrie. The thought that he had laid his hands on his wife infuriated him. Though she said he hadn't touched her sexually, he couldn't help but wonder if she was telling the truth. Gloria had been known to keep things from him.

"Hey Ella, you want to pass me up another nail?"

"Sure," she muttered and fished into a plastic bag full of them.

"You know lady stuff, right?"

Ella snorted. "Sal, my father already gave me the birds and bees talk."

"Oh no, I didn't mean that." He rested his elbow on a rung of the ladder and gazed towards the house. "I meant, you would know if someone had, well... interfered with a woman, yes?"

Her brow knit together and he regretted asking. He felt like a fool.

"Who are you talking about?"

He hesitated for a second. "Gloria."

"You want me to speak to her?"

"No. I just… well, would you?"

She smirked. "It's not a problem."

"Don't say it was me that asked. Just after she told me about Butch hitting her, I can't help think that he did something more, or maybe his brothers did. You know, with her being on this island all by herself and all."

"No, I get it. I'll bring it up when we talk about our usual, *lady stuff*," she said before chuckling. He nodded and continued beating in the last nail. Once he was done, he made his way down and took a few steps back to see if it was crooked.

"What do you think?"

She shivered, mocking him. "It's creepy alright. Let me guess, you used to do the decorations on Halloween."

He laughed a little. "Ah, I just thought we should probably look at ways of keeping people off the island, preventing people from stealing the boat, and perhaps having up some kind of alarm system."

"Beyond the security cameras?"

He hemmed and hawed. "Your father's idea is okay but let's face it, who is going to sit there and watch them day and night?"

"He would."

"Yeah, I guess you're right but no, I don't think these signs are going to cut it."

"I dunno, like you said it might keep away some. By the way, I saw the one you put on the south side." She smirked. "*Nothing inside is worth dying for?*"

"What? You can't go wrong with stringing up a firing range target with a few shots in the head. Once I added the text below it, I thought it looked pretty good."

She laughed and strolled down to the water's edge. Further down the island she saw Zach ambling along with a rifle in his hand looking out across the water.

"How's he coping?" Sal asked, following her gaze.

"Not well. He's never killed anyone before."

"Has anyone?"

"Yeah, I know what you mean but… it's like he's stuck in that moment. It wasn't his fault."

"I don't expect it was. After what's happened I don't think it will be the last person to die from a gunshot." He paused. "These are dangerous times."

She crouched down and picked up a smooth rock and skipped it out across the water.

"It doesn't seem real. All of this."

Sal pulled up beside her and stuffed his hands in his pockets. "None of us were prepared."

"My father was. Which reminds me, I appreciate all you have done for him." She skipped another rock and it bounced across the top four times before disappearing. The horizon was swallowing the sun and darkness would soon be upon them.

"Just doing my job."

"No, you went far and above what was required."

He chuckled and she shot him a sideways glance. "What?"

"I wish Gloria saw it that way. She thinks I gave too much time to your father."

"Perhaps, but look at him now. He's not reaching for the hand sanitizer every second, he's not washing his hands fifteen times a day."

"Oh, he still does that, but yeah, he's come a long way from a year ago. It still affects him and it will for some time. You have to think of it like a recovering addict. Though he might have made progress, it might only take one traumatic event to shift him back into that headspace. He finds comfort there. Some sense of peace."

Ella squinted. "Either way, thanks."

"You're welcome. Why don't you go speak to Zach? Maybe you'll cheer him up."

Sal began walking back up the embankment. Ella stood there for a few seconds more gazing out before she asked him one last question.

"Sal!"

"Yeah?" he said turning back.

"Do you think he's going to be okay?"

"Zach?"

"My father."

"Ah, you know him, he has a way of staying out of trouble."

\* \* \*

"You three are in big trouble," the cop barked at them. He'd instructed them to lie on the ground and to slide their rifles towards him. From the moment Tyrell had stepped outside, the cop was acting nervous, drifting his gun back and forth between them. Frank had put one hand out and told him to calm down but he wouldn't listen.

Slowly but surely they got to their knees and slid their guns to one side. Frank lifted his head and squinted at the cop. He was sure he had seen him before. He was young and... that's when it dawned on him.

"Wyatt?"

He stopped drifting his gun and frowned.

"It's me, Frank Talbot."

The cop looked confused but he had him hooked.

"I was with Sal Hudson. You stopped us a while back near the Sunoco gas station, after it was on fire." It still didn't appear to be registering. "Black truck. I was driving. Sal Hudson."

He gazed around nervously, then nodded. "Right, I remember now. Where's Sal?"

Frank went to get up and Wyatt screamed for him to get on the ground. This guy was super high-strung. Whatever he had eaten that morning, it wasn't doing him any good. His eyes were wide and he looked wired, as if he had consumed forty cups of coffee.

"Sorry. I just wanted to explain."

"You'll have a chance to explain behind bars."

"Um, I hate to point out the obvious but have you not seen the state of the police station?"

"I'm aware of the situation but that doesn't change anything and neither does it change the fact that you are breaking and entering into an establishment that does not belong to you."

"Okay, I've had enough of this," Tyrell said rising up to his knees.

"Get on the floor. Now!

"Put a sock in your pie hole. Listen up, deputy dipshit, maybe you didn't get the memo but we are currently experiencing a deadly pandemic. And—"

Before he could finish what he was saying, Wyatt pulled his Taser with his other hand and fired. The electrical probes hit Tyrell and he began flopping around like a fish.

"I told you."

"Hey!" Gabriel said scrambling to his feet.

"Don't make me shoot you!" Wyatt screamed aiming his firearm at him. Gabriel tossed his hands up.

"Come on, man, this is not right."

"What's not right is breaking into this place. What's not right is what the hell is going on in this town."

"Wyatt. Wyatt!" Frank shouted. He wasn't paying any attention. Wyatt had extracted the probes and had a knee on the back of one compliant Tyrell, who was now groaning.

Finally he responded. "What?" he shouted as if unable to control himself.

"Where are the other officers?"

"Gone. The two part-timers never came in for their shift, and the other officers ended up infected and the chief, well, I haven't seen him."

"So why the hell are you still doing this?"

"Because someone has to. The world might have gone to hell but nothing's changed."

"Wake up, man. Everything has changed. And if you keep this up, eventually someone is going to shoot you."

"Is that a threat?"

"No. I'm saying that others are packing just the same as us and they shoot and don't ask questions."

"Well then it's a good thing that I'm armed." He cast his gaze down at Tyrell and told him to shut up again, while he tried to figure out how to cuff him without putting his firearm away.

"Now you two, just back up."

They shifted ever so slightly.

"More. Move!"

They clambered to their feet and shifted a bit further away and watched intently as he pulled his cuffs and tried slapping them around Tyrell's wrists. Tyrell wasn't making it easy for him. He was telling him to get off and then he slid into a rant about police brutality and his skin color. All the while Frank was looking for his opening. He knew that this was absurd. All of them did. But with Wyatt packing that Glock he had to be careful. Tyrell continued to struggle and Wyatt must have figured it was pointless trying to get the cuffs on him so he yanked him up and strong-armed him over to the idling cruiser.

"Now you just stay there."

"Get your hands off me, man," Tyrell shouted kicking back.

"You keep that up and it's going to be painful for you."

"Fuck you."

Wyatt had bit off more than he could chew trying to wrestle Tyrell into the cruiser with one hand, so he slammed him on the hood of the vehicle and tried reaching for his cuffs. As hard as he tried to keep an eye on Frank and Gabriel, it was becoming almost impossible with all the kicking and yelling Tyrell was doing.

Seeing that it was a pointless endeavor, he slid the Glock into his holster so he could use both hands. That was the opening Frank was looking for. If he hadn't done that, Frank would have waited until he came and got him and then he would have turned the tables.

He couldn't reach his rifle in time but he sure as hell could plow into him. Frank burst forward and Wyatt's nostrils and eyes flared in shock as Frank dived into him and knocked him to the ground.

By the time Frank hit him, Wyatt had his hand on his gun and was struggling to get it out. They rolled around on the ground. All the while Frank was telling him to stop.

"We're not going to harm you. We just want—"

Before he could spit the words from his mouth, in Frank's peripheral vision, he saw a flash of a muzzle slip into view. Everything slowed in that moment. The barrel pressing against the officer's head — the gun going off — and a spray of red mist hitting his face.

# Chapter 14

A sharp ringing in his ears followed by disorientation was the first thing Frank felt. The next was the sound of Gabriel yelling at Tyrell. Frank squeezed his eyes shut as his body tried to return to normal.

"Why the hell did you do that?"

Frank looked up to see Gabriel slam Tyrell against the side of the cruiser. He looked down at Wyatt's motionless body. Blood covered his face and a part of his brain had seeped out. Trembling, startled, and in shock, Frank rose and backed away from the dead cop. He couldn't believe what had just happened. He immediately reached into his pocket and pulled out some wipes, and began cleaning off his face, hands, and jacket.

"He was going to take us in, maybe even kill us," Tyrell said, trying to come to his own defense. Frank flashed him one look and he put his hands up defensively. Gabriel was pacing back and forth looking at the officer then looking down the road.

"Kill us? Are you kidding?" Gabriel shouted. "The guy was just trying to do his job."

"A little late for that now," Tyrell said.

"Well it is now, you idiot." Gabriel was beside himself. Frank hadn't said a word; he was still trying to process what had happened.

"Frank, what are we gonna do?" Gabriel said in a panicked state.

Frank was crouched down at the front of the cruiser gripping the bumper and trying to get a hold of his sanity. It felt like a Mack truck had hit him. Not only was he wrestling with the fact that Tyrell had just murdered a cop and they were an accessory to it, but he had no idea if Wyatt was infected. How long had Wyatt been out in the town trying to do his job? How many people had he come in contact with? Were any of them infected? If Wyatt had the Agora virus, it would all be over for him in a matter of fourteen to twenty-four hours. Frank slammed his fist against the bumper three times in anger, and let out a yell.

The reality of this new world came crashing in and with it the harsh reality that he had already run into this issue once, at Abner's. He'd got blood on him then, but he didn't think about whether Clarence had been infected. He'd simply returned to the island. The complexity of the situation they were facing was far bigger than he thought. N-95 masks, disposable overalls, and goggles reduced the risk of contracting the virus but the only real way was to avoid people altogether. Easier said than done.

He figured he couldn't go back to the island for at least for fourteen hours, not until he had seen that he wasn't infected.

"Frank," Gabriel said stepping closer to him.

"Get back!" Frank yelled edging away. "Stay six feet away."

Gabriel got this confused look on his face and then his eyes darted to the dead officer and then back to Frank. He didn't need to explain it to him.

"We'll ride in the back of the truck."

Frank nodded.

"What if I'm infected too?" Tyrell said. "I mean he had his hands all over me. It doesn't just carry in the blood. Sweat, saliva, hell… this is messed up."

Frank looked straight at him and without missing a beat he replied, "Well if you are infected, maybe you can pass it along to Butch. At least that way you can do something good before you die."

Tyrell frowned and strolled off towards the truck. His words were harsh. He knew that. He wouldn't wish this disease on anyone, not even his worst enemy, but in the frustration of the moment he just blurted it out.

The only upside to it all was that Frank knew no police were coming to haul them away. If Wyatt was right, the others were gone, dead, or locked up behind some impenetrable door. Who knew? Before Frank got in the truck he fished out his anxiety meds and downed one. He made a note to visit one of the local pharmacies and see if he could find some more.

He took a second to calm his thoughts before he turned over the ignition and pulled out of the lot, leaving behind the cruiser and the officer. Though there was no denying that what Tyrell had done was wrong, he had to wonder where Wyatt would have taken them. The police department was in shambles. He might have thrown them in the cells but how would that have helped? There would have been no one to judge them. It was ludicrous and yet how many doctors, nurses, police officers, and military across the United States were still trying to do their jobs?

\* \* \*

It didn't take long to reach Washington Island. By the time they made it over there, it was dark and the only lights came from a crescent moon, and a canopy of stars. A few lights flickered across the water. Fire pits lit by survivors?

Jameson had told them that Washington Street went around in a circle, but one section called Gardner veered off to the right. They were to follow that road right to the end. On the left would be the home of one Vernon Red.

Most just called him Red.

*"Any gate around the place? Rabid dogs that I should be worried about?"*

*"Nothing,"* Jameson said.

*"And you say he'll remember you?"*

*"Yeah he should."*

*"Are you sure he's alive?"*

*"Oh he's alive. Probably the only one on that island that is."*

Now on any ordinary night, porch lights would have lit up the island but now it was completely dark. There weren't even any streetlights. From the moment people drove onto the island they would immediately find themselves in the small, tight-knit community. Either side of the narrow road were beautiful big homes, well-manicured gardens, and numerous bushes and pine trees.

Not a sound could be heard on the island, except from nighthawks flying overhead. Frank put the truck in neutral and just let the engine idle for a while. He glanced out his window and looked up at the two-story clapboard home. By all accounts it looked as empty as the others. Gabriel slid the rear window apart.

"You want us to go up and see?"

"Yeah, okay, but be sure to take the alcohol with you."

Frank watched the pair hop out of the truck and double-time it up the short driveway. Just down from the house was a small boathouse, and an L-shaped dock. Keeping his window down and his hand on his rifle, he listened for the first sign of trouble. He had visions of them being shot at long before they got close. He kept scanning his mirrors, paranoid of other threats.

In many ways he imagined a small community like this on the island would be able to thrive if they all worked together. It was a good distance from Clayton itself. They could create a blockage on the causeway and use their boats to reach other areas of town along the shore. And yet by the looks of the dark windows they had simply abandoned the place.

The eerie silence was shattered by the sudden sound of gunfire. One single shot. Frank burst out of the truck and sprinted up to the house. His heart was thumping in his chest as he reached the front door and found it shut. The closer he was, the clearer he could see that some of the windows had been boarded up. Hopping down off the porch he circled around back and stopped in his tracks. Gabriel was fighting with Tyrell. He cast a glance towards the house but there was no activity there.

Racing over to them, he kept his distance but shouted.

"What the hell are you doing?"

"He nearly shot me."

"I did not. I thought I saw someone in the trees," Tyrell said.

"And that gives you reason to shoot?" Gabriel spat back, while picking himself off the ground and brushing off old grass trimmings.

"Tyrell, at this rate I'm going to ban you from carrying weapons," Frank said.

"Screw both of you. You might not like it but you know what I did back there was the right thing to do."

"Right thing? That was someone's life."

He pointed to himself. "And this is mine. It's just as valuable as anyone else's and I sure as hell won't lose it to some jackass who thought he could continue on like nothing had changed."

Tyrell bent at the waist and scooped up his rifle.

"Well? Any luck?" Frank asked.

"The back door is open, I called out his name but got no response."

Frank looked up towards the house before trudging up there. "Just stay back, and put your guns away. I don't want to give him any more reason than he already has to shoot us."

He pulled a flashlight from his pocket and shone it ahead while keeping his rifle strapped to his back. The door creaked as he pushed it ever so slightly. From the silhouette of furniture inside, he could tell it led into the kitchen.

"Vernon Red. Can you hear me?" He paused. "Jameson McCready sent us. We've brought you some moonshine. We are armed but not looking to harm you. I just want to use your boat."

Still nothing.

Frank looked down at the floor. Jameson had warned him that people might use all manner of traps to prevent others from stealing. And with the door unlocked, he was taking every precaution necessary. He glanced at the floor to see if there was a board of upright nails, of course it wouldn't have been that clear. They would have covered it with a tarp or something like that but he checked anyway. It was all clear.

Looking back at the others, he motioned for them to get out of the way. He stepped to one side and gave the door a little kick with the toe of his boot, then moved back. A thud, then a creak as it swung open. No sooner had it opened another ten inches than a gun went off and blew a hole in the door. All three of them dropped to the ground and scrambled for cover. Tyrell, the trigger-happy lunatic, fired a few rounds back shattering the back windows before Frank reached him and tore the gun away.

"That's it. You're done."

Tyrell scowled. "Why? He fired first."

"We're trying to communicate with the guy. Firing back isn't going to get us shit."

"So you're taking it away permanently?"

"Call it a timeout," Gabriel said with a grin. "Once you've learned to act like a responsible big boy, you'll get it back."

Frank smirked. They were positioned behind a bush just a few feet from the porch. He imagined Vernon would tell them to get the fuck off his property but there was only silence.

"I don't see why we can't just go down and steal the boat?"

"We could, or we could do the decent thing and actually ask the guy to use it. Hell, after having nearly got our head shot off back at the distillery, I think we've broken enough laws for one evening."

Tyrell snorted. "Laws. There are none now. You two need to wake up and smell the coffee. This is a dog-eat-dog world and only the strongest are going to survive."

"Would you just shut the hell up?" Gabriel said.

After five minutes of waiting for something to happen, Frank indicated for Gabriel to go around the side while he went around the other.

"Whatever you do, don't shoot the bastard. There's been enough killing for one day."

He nodded and while staying low to the ground dashed off, using the shadows of the trees to keep him well hidden.

"You can come with me."

"But you're infected. I mean, you might be."

"And so might you. Now let's go," Frank replied.

They moved stealthily up the side of the house and peered through the windows but it was pitch-dark inside. It didn't make sense. Who would sit in the dark waiting for someone to show up?

"Wait here, I'm going back up there."

His pulse was racing and he was trying his best to remain calm but he was anything but calm. Frank slid back onto the porch and made his way to the back door. This time he got down real low and instead of sticking his head around the corner he reached for a cushion off the porch rocker and tossed it through the doorway. He heard it land and slide but there was no reaction shot. There should have been a reaction shot. It was human nature under anxiety-fueled conditions. Perhaps he hadn't seen it.

"Red! Can you hear me? We are not here to harm you. I just want to talk."

He took another pillow and tossed it. Nothing. Not a peep, or even a creak of a floorboard. Something was not right. Still nervous he pulled his flashlight and took a piece of the shattered glass and cast his light upon it at an angle, and then positioned it by the door. He moved it back and forth until he saw it. He snorted. Clever.

"Tyrell. Gabriel."

"Yep," he heard him a short distance away.

"Let's go."

He rose up off the ground and brushed himself off

before cautiously stepping into the house and moving off to the right. Positioned a few feet from the door and duct-taped to a chair was a sawed-off shotgun. A piece of string went from the trigger to some kind of mechanism that engaged the gun the moment the door was opened.

"I always thought you had to pull the door for that to work."

"Obviously not."

Frank shone his light from the door handle over several cogs down to the metal contraption. It used some kind of release-and-tighten mechanism. He had to wonder if Jameson had built it for Red. What other surprises awaited them inside?

Gabriel was the closest to the light switch.

"You want to turn that on," Tyrell said. Gabriel reached fro the switch.

"No," Frank immediately said. "Don't touch anything. Who knows what else this guy has rigged up?"

They moved through the house using their flashlights until Gabriel called out.

"Eh, Frank. You might want to come and take a look at this."

Frank was holding a photograph that contained some family picture. Something he'd learned fast in times like these was that family took on new meaning. You began to appreciate every moment, as there was no way of knowing if it would be the last. Frank headed up the stairs taking two at a time until he reached a doorway that Tyrell was standing in. Inside was a large bedroom with a four-poster bed. The first thing he noticed was the smell of vomit. Lying in the middle of the bed with several empty bottles of alcohol around him, along with sleeping pills, was Red. A small amount of vomit was on the side of his pillow but beyond that he looked as if he had just gone to sleep.

Frank exhaled hard.

"Well, there goes what Jameson said about him being alive for sure," Tyrell scoffed.

It went to show that just because a person could survive, it didn't mean they wanted to. No doubt he was one of many that had decided to take their own life rather than suffer some painful existence. The power grid was functioning but for how long? How long before supplies would run out? Red's death taught Frank a valuable lesson. It didn't matter how many supplies a person had gathered. It didn't matter how many people they had around them, or how isolated they were. If they weren't mentally ready to deal with it, they wouldn't last.

Before they exited the house, they made sure there was no one else inside. After making their way down to his private boat dock, Frank looked at Gabriel.

"You sure you want to do this? If you don't, tell me now and we'll head back. I'm going to have to stay here on the mainland for the evening."

"I'm in, no worries there. Listen, why don't you come over with us? Perhaps we can be a distraction while you check the place out."

"No, they are bound to have people keeping an eye on the surrounding waters."

"Grindstone is a hell of a lot bigger than your island, Frank. He'd need a whole army. Besides, look at the size of that boat. I'm sure you can find somewhere to hide on it," Gabriel said.

Frank blew out his cheeks and gazed out across the inky waters. With him knowing how to navigate the river, and it being so dark, it was an option. If he didn't go with them, he'd only be kicking around on Washington Island and who knew if there were others that had heard them arrive. It could be more trouble than it was worth. At least this way he could keep an eye on the two and find out what was going on with the other islanders. There had to be more than just Butch's family over there.

"Alright. We'll go together."

"Just one thing," Tyrell harped up and pointed at him. "I will get that gun back, right?"

"Just get in the boat."

## Chapter 15

Dodge Memorial Center, or otherwise referred to as Dodge Hall, wasn't much to look at. A rectangular building with grey siding and a brown roof, it had for many years been used for all manner of community events, including a square dance on Saturday nights. Often they brought in a local DJ or band. However, as Butch stood before the small crowd he was in no mood for fun or games.

"Where are the others?" he barked at Joey.

"Dougie and Bret are still trying to find folks."

"They've left?"

"No, they are on the island somewhere."

He shook his head in bewilderment. Trying to get them all to meet at the hall was harder than wrangling pigs. He would rather done that, at least then he wouldn't have had to deal with these imbeciles.

At the far end of the room attached to the wall was the

American flag. All around the walls were framed photos of people and places on the island from times gone by. Many were black-and-white. Butch stood behind a makeshift pulpit like a minister about to give a sermon. He was tapping his fingers impatiently and gazed out at the many scared faces that looked back at him.

After ten minutes, he was about done waiting.

"Right, listen up, I'm not going to wait any longer. I've invited you all here—"

"Invited? I had a gun shoved in my face," a man cut him off.

"That's only because you got belligerent with me," Misty replied.

"Settle down," Butch said, giving a waving motion with his hand. "It's important that you are here tonight because there has been a turn of events and… well… as long as you are on this island and enjoying the perks of its safety, you are obligated to attend any and all meetings. So having said that let me address specifics."

He was just about to begin when Dougie and Bret

stumbled into the room. He squeezed his eyes shut and tried to push down his desire to react.

"Finally."

"Sorry about that, we had a couple who were busy eating," Dougie held up a large bag.

"That's ours."

Butch stepped down off the platform and walked to the back of the room. Dougie and Bret pushed the couple forward, and then Dougie emptied the contents of the pillowcase out onto the floor. A bunch of cans rattled as they rolled out, along with several packages of beef jerky, chips, candy bars, and bags of rice.

Butch stared at it all and picked out some jerky. "Well look at that. So where was this bag?"

"They had it hidden in their boat."

"Hidden stash. I like that. However, we can't be having you doing that. No, that's not going to work. You know why?"

There was no answer by the couple.

"Look around you. There are many mouths to feed on

this island. Now if you are not sharing what you have, it means you are taking for granted every single one of these people."

The young guy stepped forward. He was a gangly man with round glasses and a bald spot on top of his head. He couldn't have been more than twenty-seven. "Listen, Butch, we didn't mean anything by it. In fact, I forgot we had this."

"Yeah," his spouse said. "It's just a misunderstanding."

"Really? That's good to know. You see, because I would hate to think that you were both taking for granted my good nature in allowing you to stay on this island. You see what I was about to say tonight affects you and your lovely... what's your name again?"

"Karla."

"Karla, that's it. And you're..."

He turned to the young guy.

"Mitch."

He let out a chuckle. "Mitch, Butch. Hey... you think we might be related?"

He eyed him with a devilish grin. Butch loved playing with folks. In his time running the store, he enjoyed instilling fear into the folks who came in to buy items. It was how he got a lot of people in Clayton to sign up to his retreats. He would talk about the worse-case scenarios. The great what-if… and sure enough he could get some of the most worried folks eating out of his hand. By the time they walked out of his shop, not only had they bought more than they came in for but they had signed up to one of his retreats.

As he looked around, he even had a few of them still with him as friends.

"I don't see the resemblance," the man said, not fully getting the joke.

"Well listen up, Mitch and Karla. As much as I don't like to punish people, I mean, it's not really my place to do that but being as you are on my soil, essentially in my house, that means you were eating my food without my permission. So, there has to be some consequences." He walked around them, touching them on the shoulder like a lion toying with its prey. "Now to be honest with you, I really haven't thought too much yet about what kind of consequences there are going to be for those who stay here and fall out of line."

The man immediately came to his girl's defense. "Karla didn't have anything to do with it. I knew about the food. I told her and well... if you want me to go without food for a day, then, sure that's fine."

Butch stared at him blankly and then burst into laughter. "Go without food for a day?" The others began to laugh slowly, a nervous chuckle broke out among them all. "Why would I make you go without food for a day? You must really think I'm a monster."

Mitch chuckled along with him.

"No, you will get to eat. So will the lovely Karla. But eh," he bit down on his bottom lip and looked out one of the windows into the darkness. "I think Karla will stay with me tonight."

"What?"

"You know. We'll get a little acquainted. You don't

mind, do you, Misty?"

"Not at all." Misty came over and rubbed her fingers across her lips and eyed Karla like a ripe fruit.

"But I…" Mitch spluttered.

Butch leaned into him and whispered into his ear. "Some punishment is only understood when it happens to those that we love. You took something that I value, so now I'm going to take something of value of yours. But don't worry, I'll return it in the morning."

"No. No, this is…"

Before he could spit the words out, Dusty slammed him in the gut with the butt of his rifle. Mitch coughed hard and fell to his knees. Karla tried to move to his side but was hauled back by Joey.

"Take her back to the house."

The next few minutes were filled with screams as Joey dragged her out of there and Mitch attempted to stop them. Butch motioned to Dusty and Bret to take him outside and keep him quiet.

The rest of the islanders in the hall looked on in

horror. A couple got up to protest but as soon as a weapon was flashed they sat back down. Butch knew the others wanted to say something but none of them had the guts to speak up out of fear of something far worse happening to them.

The fact was he wasn't going to lay a hand on Karla, and neither would any of his brothers or cousins. They weren't rapists but a person in his position needed to know how to work a room. It was all about appearances. If he did nothing, the others would have stepped out of line and then he would have people turning against him.

No, that wasn't happening. He was at the helm of this ship and he'd take them all down with him before he handed over the reins.

"Now, where was I?" And just like that he moved back into what he was about to say without skipping a beat. "It's come to my attention that a rogue group of men are killing people over on the mainland to get what they want. Of course, this is very disturbing."

"How different is that from what you're doing?"

"Geesh, do I really have to rehash this again? We are sharing what we have here on the island. We haven't taken anything that won't be fairly distributed back to you. In return you get to avoid all the shit that is going on over on the mainland. And, in the event those assholes try to come over here, we will protect you. That's right. We will protect you. Am I making myself clear?"

He eyed the man called Landon Forester with a look of mistrust. He'd been one of the few that had kicked up a fuss when they began doing the rounds on the island. He and his wife, Sandra, were two he was going to have to keep close tabs on. He couldn't have anyone rocking the boat. Couldn't these people understand what he was trying to do here? Someone had to govern this island, ensure the safety of those on it, and make sure that no one took advantage of anyone else. If that meant he looked like the bad guy, well he was more than willing to wear that badge.

"So we are going to need a lot more cooperation around here."

"Like?" Landon asked.

"Like taking shifts and watching out for any strangers on the island. If anyone shows up at your home, you are to let us know right away."

"Shifts?" Landon asked again in a defiant tone.

*This guy is starting to piss me off,* Butch thought as he moved a little closer to see if it would intimidate him. As a large man, he'd had little trouble with people arguing with him. Those who tried to push their luck were swiftly given a backhand, even if they didn't deserve it. The key was to strike first and not give them a chance to get to the point where they thought they could take him. But by the looks of Landon, that wasn't going to be required. Landon edged back in his seat and he got this, oh shit, perhaps I shouldn't have said that look on his face.

"Yes. Everyone is going to take a turn in patrolling the island, day and night. There is a lot of land to cover."

"And are you going to give us ATV's?"

"If you have them you can use them otherwise God's given you two legs."

Butch continued to walk the full length of the building. He pushed his chest out with a sense of pride. There was something to be said for governing people. It was like his own tiny state, and he got to make the rules. He imagined that many of the people in the country detested this new strain of virus that was sweeping the land but not him. It was giving him the world that he had always wanted. One in which the playing field was leveled. One in which he got to use all the survival skills he had learned and taught over the years. And ultimately it gave him the opportunity to have men respect and fear him. That kind of shit couldn't be bought. Honestly, he didn't care whether people feared him or respected him but they would all come to thank him.

He turned his back for a moment and then twisted around. "Oh, and another thing, you will all go on runs with us to collect more items from the mainland."

"Will you be sharing?" Landon said with a smirk on his face.

"Have you been beyond this island?"

"Not since this kicked off."

"Then you don't know what it's like out there. We do. And if you want to survive the coming winter, and maybe even the following year, you will do what is asked of you."

"Asked?" someone else piped up. "We're being asked. That's the first I've heard."

A few agreed and grumbled.

Perhaps Landon's attitude was beginning to rub off on the others. He hadn't thought about that. Maybe getting them all together was a bad idea. It allowed for a mob mindset to form. Landon sat back in his seat and folded his arms. Was that an unspoken form of communication? A giant fuck you? Was he sending a message to him that he wasn't going to do jack squat? Oh, he was going to have words with him before this night was out.

Butch was about to discuss another concern when the doors swung open and Palmer and Jackson pushed forward two men, one white and one black, into the midst of them.

"And who do we have here?" Butch said with a smile

on his face.

## Chapter 16

Sal glanced at his wristwatch, then stared through the night vision binoculars. The St. Lawrence River was lit up by a luminescent green. He scanned the horizon looking for any sign of him. A few distant lights twinkled. Survivors, he thought.

"He should have been back by now."

"Perhaps they ran into some difficulty locating Red," Jameson said while lighting up a cigarette.

"There can't be more than twenty houses on that island, and only one Gardner Street. How difficult could it be?"

"Well, there's nothing we can do. Without that boat, we are stranded."

It was just after eight-thirty at night. Frank had made it clear that he was going to get them safely to Red's and then return. He didn't anticipate being any longer than a few hours. While Sal didn't think it was cause for alarm, as there could have been any number of reasons why he was delayed, he was also a realist and nervous after their run-in with the Guthries.

"This was a dumb idea," Sal said. "I should have gone with him."

"A voice of reason?"

"Exactly."

"He's a grown ass man for God's sake, Sal. I think he can handle this."

"I don't know about that."

Jameson scoffed. "You've spent so much time with him you have Stockholm syndrome."

"What on earth are you on about?"

"Gloria says you and him are like two peas in a pod. She's tempted to call you the Odd Couple."

He grumbled as he continued gazing through the binoculars like a father looking for his prodigal son. The reality was, there was an element of truth in that. He had never worked so closely with a client. Initially it had started like any other business relationship. He hit the clock at the start of their sessions and was out the door one minute after. It wasn't like he hadn't dealt with others who had the same kind of OCD but something about Frank intrigued him. Slowly, over time it became like a personal challenge and morphed into almost an obsession to see him cured of his phobia. Then of course there was the time they spent on the road heading to Queens. They had formed a bond that could only be forged through traumatic experiences. He didn't see him like a son, as he wasn't much older than him. More like a brother. The brother he never had. Of course, he would never tell Gloria that. She would have climbed the walls and probably told him to go and move in with him. He ground his teeth.

If he was honest, in some ways Frank had helped him perhaps more than he had helped Frank. Up until he had met Frank, he had taken a very placid approach to life. The comment about Gloria wearing the pants wasn't far from the truth. In his entire marriage, he had never spoken back to her. Not that he didn't want to, but it just wasn't something he was used to seeing.

Sal's father hadn't been a psychiatrist. He was a blue-collar worker who had worked for the railroad. He worked long hours and when he was home, he generally didn't like to be disturbed. His mother would bring him his supper while he watched TV and Sal was lucky if he managed to get a word out of him. When the last freight service ended in 1972, his father lost his job and after that he struggled to get work and spiraled down into deep depression. He was never the same man after that. It was as if his entire identity was wrapped up in his career.

Though he suffered in silence, he never once took it out on Sal's mother. Not once did he raise his voice and there was something about that Sal admired. Others might have said he needed to grow a pair but he didn't think his father was lacking in confidence. He simply showed a great deal of respect for his mother. In many ways, his observations of his father were what led him to want to understand people. It could be said it drove him into his current line of work as a psychiatrist.

Yeah, it was from those early days he had formed his ideas about how he was to speak to women. Don't talk back. Don't raise your voice. Don't rock the boat. And though it made for a peaceful life, he always felt as though he had repressed a small part of himself. Frank however was a different kettle of fish. He spoke up for himself, raised his voice, and rocked the boat, perhaps to his own detriment. Though Frank might have said it cost him his marriage, Sal didn't think that was the case. It took two to tango and his conversations with Kate led him to believe that she had a few issues of her own.

Sal cast a glance back towards the cottage. The light was on in the kitchen and he could see Gloria puttering around. Though he had only raised his voice a few times over the past year, he had to wonder if the problems in his marriage had stemmed from her wanting him to take more of a lead. To speak out. To stand up. To give her some grain to rub up against. *Iron refines iron*, his old college teacher would tell him.

Had he been iron to her? He couldn't say he had. His

approach had always been to take a back seat, whereas Frank took the bull by the horns.

Jameson snapped his fingers in front of Sal's face. "Sal. You there, buddy?"

"What?" Sal drifted out of his daze-like state.

"I thought I lost you there for a moment."

"Sorry, just thinking about the past."

"Don't we all," Jameson said, tossing the remainder of his smoked cigarette. Golden embers glowed for a second until it hit the water. "Look, I think we should probably head in. He'll be back. There's nothing we can do right now."

"Yeah, I suppose so."

He hesitated before following him into the house.

* * *

Gabriel's eyes drifted over the rabble squeezed into the small hall. His heart was pounding. From the moment he saw the AK47s the men were carrying, he had begun to have second thoughts about agreeing to do this. After reaching the shore, they hid their rifles nearby and headed towards the nearest house. Frank told them that he would be watching and that if anything went wrong, he would do his utmost to get them out of it. Though it was comforting to know, words meant very little now. What chance did he stand against them?

A thick bearded man, roughly the same height as Gabriel but much larger in width, approached them while the others stood back and manned the doors.

"And who might you be?"

"Gabriel, and this is Tyrell, a friend of mine."

The man observed them, looking them up and down and studying them as if trying to determine what to do.

He sniffed hard. "Where you from?"

They had already agreed that they would say Watertown; any mention of Queens might have struck a chord with Butch and given him a reason to doubt their story.

"Watertown. Things have got real bad down there and so we were hoping to get away from the chaos."

"And you chose my island?"

Tyrell looked around at the people. "Seemed as good as any other."

"But you chose mine?" he said.

Gabriel nodded. With every second that passed he was hoping that Tyrell didn't start waffling. Frank had told him to leave the talking to Gabriel, something to which he took offense.

They both nodded. "We're not looking for any trouble, just a warm bed for the night, perhaps a hot meal until we can decide where to go next."

"So you are moving on?"

"We haven't exactly decided," Tyrell said.

"I'm Butch by the way, Butch Guthrie." He extended his hand and Gabriel noted how hard he squeezed when he shook it. There was a look of superiority in his eyes as if he was trying to intimidate or make it clear who was in charge.

"Pleased to meet you."

"You were in Clayton for a while?"

"A few hours until we could find a boat."

"A boat? Where is it?" He turned to one of the two men who had brought them in.

They shrugged. "They just walked up on us."

Butch breathed in deeply, clasped his hands behind his back, and walked back to the makeshift pulpit on a step further down before returning.

"Look, if it's a bother we can leave," Gabriel said. He didn't like the awkward silence or the way Butch was staring at his men. It seemed as if they were trying to determine their fate. His eyes darted to the window and the darkness beyond. Was Frank watching? Did he have Butch in his crosshairs?

"No. No, you are guests. Please, take a seat. We were just wrapping up here."

They took a seat close to a couple but clearly by the looks Butch's men were giving them, they didn't trust them one bit.

Butch returned to his spot and continued discussing the needs of the island and how everyone would have an opportunity to serve. The guy made it sound like he was king and it was an honor to be his bitch.

* * *

Frank lurked in the darkness with his rifle on the ready. He had contemplated the idea of taking out Butch from a distance. It would have been so easy. Waiting for him to emerge and then having Gabriel distract him while he lined up Butch's fat head in his sight. One shot and the others would just disperse like cowards.

But as much as he had churned it over in his mind, he couldn't bring himself to do it. He wasn't a murderer. He'd killed people before but that was war, it was justified at least in his eyes. He was serving his country.

He couldn't justify killing a man who had simply stolen what he had. Sure he had slapped Gloria, but hell, there were tons of people who wanted to give her a slap. She had a way of getting under anyone's skin. Not that he would have done it. He abhorred violence against women but she certainly knew how to press people's buttons.

No, he had told them to get in, find out what they could, and leave the island at the first chance they got, or the first sign of trouble.

After watching them go into the hall and lingering a while in the shadows, he had decided to take advantage of the time he had and check out the Guthries' residence. Initially the idea was to have the two guys do it but with him on the island it just made sense to use them as a distraction. He figured not all of the Guthrie family would be at the hall but at least he might be able to figure out where the supplies were.

Frank moved from his position. It was pitch-dark and without the use of his flashlight, and no streetlights on the island, he had to use the natural light from the moon and his memory of previous visits to the island as a means of making his way to Guthrie's property.

As he was trudging along, he decided to make use of the time to call Kate. He hadn't spoken to her in several days. Every time he tried to get through he either got a busy line or her voicemail, which was full. As he pulled his phone out, the charge was weak but not as bad as the signal. It kept flittering between two bars and one, and then none. Great, he thought.

But that wasn't the only thing that caught his attention. He'd received four text messages from Sal. Then it dawned on him that he had told him he would be returning by eight. It was nine-fifteen now. He checked the messages and shot him back an update.

He hadn't taken but a few steps before another one came back.

*Damn it, Frank. Now how the hell do we get off this island and help you, if you get into trouble?*

He had a point. But what Sal didn't realize was that he had got Wyatt's blood on him and he wasn't sure whether he was infected or not. Did he tell him? Sal knew Wyatt, it was the right thing to do, yet on the other hand he didn't want to cause panic, especially for Ella. Nothing could be worse than to be stranded on an island with no means of escape and discovering your parent had possibly, maybe, contracted the Agora virus.

Another text message came in from Sal and he knew he wasn't going to be able to dance around the issue. Sal knew him better than that.

*I can't come back for twenty-four hours. Please don't tell Ella.*

That was all he said. All he needed to say, Sal would understand. Wouldn't he?

No further messages from him was either a good sign or it meant that Sal had switched into psychiatrist mode and was about to give him a mini-lecture on remaining calm via text message.

Then one finally came in.

*Understood. Stay safe.*

That was it. He had dodged the bullet. At least he thought he had. Continuing to trudge through the brambles and dense undergrowth he picked up the pace and broke into a jog. Anyone who had lived in Clayton all their life had at some point visited Grindstone Island. Though it was the fourth biggest of the Thousand Islands, it didn't take long to navigate it.

He was grateful for the cover of night and the thick hemlock, pine, and cedar trees that shrouded his silhouette. As he broke across a trail and on into another section of woodland, he heard a motor and saw headlights coming his way. He ducked down and got real low to the ground. Had he been spotted? Had they forced Gabriel to tell the truth? The growl of an ATV shot by him, heading in the direction of the hall. He waited another thirty seconds before jumping to his feet and heading in the direction of where the ATV came from. It took him close to fifteen minutes to reach the lit-up property. He'd seen the yellow lights in the trees and heard music playing loudly. As he got close to the tree line he could make out a blazing fire in the middle of a fire pit and three people sitting around in chairs.

"You know if he catches you drinking beers, he'll have your ass on a stick," a woman said. He couldn't make out who she was but he knew the guy. It was Bret. Bret Guthrie was the only one of the family that seemed ordinary. Frank swore that he'd been adopted. The guy beside him was Joey, Butch's cousin.

Frank pulled his Glock 22, stayed close to the tree line,

and moved in on the house.

## Chapter 17

As Frank got closer to the house, the more on edge he felt. What the hell was he doing? Creeping around in the night with a weapon in his hand. Was he really going to use it? He had to keep telling himself to stay calm. Don't lose your cool. Too many times in Iraq he had seen guys lose their shit when pushed into a tight corner. It didn't matter how much training a jarhead had, or how many years they had pined over the idea of becoming a marine, all that was swept aside when they found themselves smack bang in the middle of a desert with bullets flying over their head. No amount of training could prepare a person for that.

He edged his way out of a cluster of pine trees and made a beeline for the rear door of the oversized home. He could hear laughter inside but couldn't tell how many were there. Staying in the shadows he hugged the wall with his back and peered through the window. In the middle of the living room, there were several people he didn't recognize. He turned and moved along the wall going in the opposite direction. As he reached the corner he saw an entrance for a side porch, he gave it a try and it opened. They obviously weren't expecting visitors. No alarm went off. Sliding inside he found himself in what appeared to be a greenhouse for growing vegetables. As he gazed around at the tables covered in produce and different plants in various states of growth, he shook his head. It was disappointing to think that Butch felt the need to raid his place. How many others had he done this to? How many others were going without their basic needs because of him? Meanwhile he was flourishing with more than enough.

Right then, he heard voices and someone drawing near. Frank ducked under one of the many wooden tables that lined the sides, and squeezed behind several bags of fertilizer. He did his best to cover his entire body as boots pounded the floor, and got closer.

"Get me a beer as well," a voice cried out.

"I'd like to see the day you get off your ass and get me one for once."

It was Bret. Tucked behind multiple bags and in the heat of the greenhouse, he was sweating buckets. The door opened and in came Bret mumbling under his breath about how tired he was of taking their shit. He ambled over to a mini-fridge and pulled out several bottles of beer. Then he started looking around with a scowl on his face.

"Oh come on, where is it?"

He moved across the room heading in the direction of where Frank was. Clutching his Glock he turned it outward, preparing for the worst. He wanted to close his eyes and pretend he wasn't there but he was and if Bret dropped down to knee level, the chances were he would see him. The bags partially covered him but it wasn't perfect.

"Bret, hurry up, we don't have long before he'll be expecting us back."

"I'm coming, hold your horses," he shouted. After, he

went back to saying what an asshole Joey was, and how he wished he'd headed east to his uncle's place in Maine. It was to be expected. Not everyone would be onboard with Butch.

"There it is," he said. That was followed by the noise of metal and then the hiss of bottle tops being opened. Frank heard him open two and then was waiting for the third when the bottle opener clattered on the floor. Bret cursed and reached down to grab it. Frank's eyes flared as he saw his face come into view. He wasn't looking directly at him but to the side as he tried to reach underneath and grab it.

"Bret! Come on."

"Fuck sake," Bret yelled.

He stood up and smacked his head and then the air was filled with curse words as he walked off with the bottles.

Frank waited a couple of seconds until he was gone before he slipped out and dashed towards the door that led into the house. As soon as he slipped in, he crouched down and listened for voices, footsteps, or any sign of activity that would determine where he shouldn't head. He started making his way towards the kitchen, figuring there might be a large pantry or some kind of storage unit built into the house to keep everything in but he had only made it a few feet when the patter of kids' feet could be heard against tiles. Before he had a chance to rush into a nearby room, a young girl shot out into the corridor. She had bright wide blue eyes, and couldn't have been more than six years of age. She glanced at Frank and for a moment it felt as if his heart had stopped. It was only when she went on her way without even saying a word that he realized he'd been holding his breath. He continued on down the hallway. The sound of someone else approaching made him veer right and head for the basement.

The very second he was inside he kept his ear to the door and waited until they went by. Deciding he would wait a little longer, he slowly descended the stairs until he was down inside a finished basement. The guy had really coughed up a lot of money to do the place up. It was kitted out with leather couches, a huge wide-screen TV, and then his eyes fell upon stacks of MRE boxes from the floor to the ceiling.

*That bastard has more than enough.*

He wandered down the full length of the basement that was one long corridor with multiple bedrooms on either side. He checked inside each one. It was like the lap of luxury. This was a prepper who hadn't cut corners.

When he reached the fourth room he noticed it was locked. Bingo. There were only a few reasons they would lock a room and he assumed it had to have been where all the good shit was stashed. He paused a second, thinking he heard something. When there was no sound he pulled his knife and tried prying the door open but the sucker wouldn't budge. He had no lock kit on him. He had noticed a key rack on the ground floor when he came in, but he knew he wasn't going to find the right key in time. He pressed on and checked a few more rooms. Some of them were stocked up with bags of grain, and cans of alcohol. As he sorted through it to see if any of it was his, he heard someone cough further down the hall. That was followed by a female's voice.

"You can't keep me in here."

He frowned and ducked back out into the corridor.

"I can hear you out there," she continued.

Frank tossed a glance back up the corridor before he moved in the direction of the room.

"If you think you are going to get away with this you are sorely mistaken. The police might not be in Clayton but they sure as hell are in the larger cities. I'm going to report all of you."

Frank hesitated before he tried the door. When it opened, he was surprised to find a woman laying on the ground with both her hands in cuffs around a pipe. She had dirty blond hair, and her cheeks were red from crying.

"Well? Are you just going to stand there?"

Frank looked over his shoulder before entering and closing the door behind him.

She cowered back as much as she could. "You touch me, I'll scream."

He put a finger up to his lips and crouched down to her level.

"I'm not with them."

She studied his face for a moment as if to determine whether he was a threat or not.

"How do I know that?"

He didn't recognize her from the town, though it had grown over the years and he had spent far too much time hidden away from society, only coming out when he needed to get the basics.

He pulled out a knife and her nostrils flared in terror.

"Help," she screamed at the top of her voice.

He immediately pressed his hand over her mouth to keep her quiet. Right then he heard someone shout down.

"You better shut up or I'll come down there."

Her eyes bulged above his hand as he kept it firmly in place. The last thing he needed now was to have to deal with one of Butch's family.

"Listen, I'll get you out of here but I need you to keep it down." He stared at her. "Now I'm going to take my hand off your mouth, you aren't going to scream, okay?"

She nodded affirmatively. He released his grip, and then looked at her hair for a bobby pin but there wasn't one. There were two ways of getting handcuffs off if someone didn't have a key. As he didn't have a key or a bobby pin he did the next best thing.

"I'll be right back."

"Don't leave me."

"I'm just going to a room a few feet from here. I promise I'll be right back."

She didn't look convinced but he left nevertheless. Carefully and quickly he moved down to the room where he'd seen the grain and beer cans. He went in and retrieved one of the cans and darted back into the room where the woman was.

"What's your name by the way?"

"Karla."

"Karla. Frank."

She gave a slight smile but it was clear she just wanted to get the hell out of there.

He emptied the contents down the sink and then tore the can apart. Using his knife he cut out a piece of the thin metal into a rectangular shape. Then he crouched down beside her and placed one end of the torn-off metal into the gap that was close to the teeth. The flat metal slid down into the cuff, and once he had it down there, he told her to turn her wrist. As soon as she did that, her hand came free. A look of shock, perhaps gratitude spread across her face. She pulled the other cuff around the bar, it dangled from her hand and she was about to get up when they heard boots coming down the hall.

"Shit, put them back on."

"No, I…"

"Do it now or we are both dead."

Reluctantly she resumed the position she was in and locked her hand back in place. The rooms were small. A bed, a small washroom with a sink and toilet, and room for a closet. The closet wasn't big enough for him, and he certainly wouldn't be able to fit under the bed. The only place he could hide was in the washroom behind the door. It meant the door would be slightly open as there was little room inside but he had no other option. The sound of boots came closer. He heard the main door swing open. He'd told Karla not to look at him but to keep looking forward.

"What the hell was all that racket about?" a gruff voice barked.

"You can't keep me in here."

"Lady, we can do whatever the hell we want."

Frank couldn't tell who it was only that it was a male.

"You need to use the washroom?"

"No."

"Then why were you yelling?"

When she didn't reply, he must have seen that as some odd indication that she had made a whole bunch of noise to get him down there so she could put moves on him.

"Ah, I know what you're after. Well hey darling, you should have just said. But here's the thing, I can't take you out of those cuffs, so we'll just have to improvise."

Frank heard a pant zipper go down and a belt buckle come loose. Then the guy stepped toward the cramped bathroom and shoved against the door. When it bounced back, he heard him mutter. "What the hell?"

As he stuck his head around to take a look, Frank cracked him with a right hook and he stumbled back against the wall. Before he could let out a yell, Frank grabbed him and twisted him over and put his arm around his neck in a chokehold. Pushing his feet up against the wall and leaning back against the other wall, he used all the force he had to put that guy out but he was struggling like a fish out of water. He didn't want to kill him. That wouldn't just change the dynamics of everything; it would send him on a course to becoming something he wasn't — a cold-blooded murderer.

As much as he tried to choke him out, Joey held on to his arm for dear life. It was when he began slamming his foot against the wall that Frank knew he was running out of time. Any minute now they would hear him and someone would come down.

What didn't help the issue was Karla was trying to kick him in the stomach with her feet.

"Karla, enough."

Slowly but surely, Joey lost consciousness. His limbs went limp and he was snoring up a storm. Frank lifted a hand for a second thinking he had heard something. He dashed over to the door and looked out down the corridor. Thankfully, no one had heard his stomping. The music outside took care of that.

He rushed back into the room and unshackled Karla. When she got up she gave Joey another kick.

"Karla."

"You can't leave him alive. He'll tell the others."

In that moment he knew he had two choices. Cuff Joey to the basin, or kill him. Either one would still cause Butch to hunt them down. He stared down at the unconscious cousin for a second and then pulled out his knife.

# Chapter 18

After the meeting concluded, Butch waited until those inside had dispersed before he approached Gabriel and Tyrell. He scratched the back of his head while he looked at them as if trying to decide whether they were going to be a problem.

Gabriel figured they had a fifty-fifty chance of surviving.

Butch squinted at them both. "So you need a bed for the night?"

They nodded.

"Why didn't you stay on the boat?"

"I get seasick," Tyrell said immediately.

"Fair enough. We'll let you stay the night, give you something to eat but it's not free. What do you have on you?"

"Just the clothes on our back."

"What about the boat?"

"Life jackets. Boat stuff."

Butch pursed his lips and narrowed his eyes at them. "You sure you're from Watertown?"

"I'd show you ID but I left in a hurry and didn't take my wallet with me."

"Is that so?"

Tyrell shrugged. "Yeah."

He gave them back a toothy grin. "Then it's going to cost you." He tapped Palmer beside him while not taking his eyes off them for even a second. "What do you say, Palmer? What's one night's rent, supper, and breakfast go for nowadays?"

"I don't know, boss. But it's not cheap. Supply, demand, and whatnot."

"Good point. It's hard to come by a safe, virus-free bed and a warm meal." Butch sniffed hard and looked them up and down. "You boys look strong. I could use a few more strong men. So here's what I'm going to do, you work for me for a couple of days, and I'll take the boat you came over on and we'll call it even."

"Are you serious?" Tyrell blurted out, only to get elbowed in the side by Gabriel.

"Oh I don't screw around when it comes to business. Now the question is, boys, do we have a deal?"

"Are you out of your mind?" Tyrell replied.

"What my friend was trying to saying," Gabriel glared at Tyrell, "is that we need that boat."

"Don't we all?"

Palmer, Jackson, and Butch all let out a laugh, as though they were privy to some inside joke.

"We'll work for you for three days. But you have to feed us and give us a bed for those days."

"Oh I think you have this all backwards. One night's rent plus food is worth two day's work."

"Then where would we sleep on the second day?" Tyrell said with a degree of hostility.

"Your boat, under the stars." Butch shrugged. "Who cares?"

"It's not exactly a fair exchange."

"We're not living in fair times."

Gabriel breathed in deeply and put his arm around Tyrell. He put up one finger. "Do you mind if I have a word with my friend here?"

"Sure, go ahead but you might want to speed it up, I hear we are having barbecued ribs for dinner tonight. And I do like me some ribs."

Gabriel wandered to the back of the room and kept his voice down low. He peered over his shoulder at Butch and the others who were smirking.

"What are you doing?" Gabriel asked.

"The guy is shafting us on this deal."

"We're not even going to be here three days, remember." Gabriel's eyes flared in an attempt to indicate the obvious. Chances were they would be able to find wherever all the supplies were being stored in the first day.

"Well of course we aren't. Hell, I've seen sleazy fifty-dollar motels on skid row give better deals than this crook."

Gabriel shook his head. "Just let me do the talking.

I'm pretty sure that's what Frank said."

They walked back over to them and Butch stood there with his thumbs hooked into his waistband like he was the sheriff of some old Wild West town.

"So, boys, do we have a deal?"

Gabriel put his hand out and Butch gripped it hard. "Very good. So, tell us about yourselves."

If he was as bad as Frank made him out to be, he certainly was doing a poor job of meeting their expectation. So far all they'd seen was someone who liked to swindle people.

They walked out of the building and over to a collection of ATV's.

"You can ride with Jackson and Palmer."

Gabriel jumped on the back with Jackson and the throaty ATV roared to life. He cast one more glance at Tyrell before the vehicle lunged forward and wet dirt spat up behind them like a rooster's tail.

* * *

Down in the basement, Frank leaned over Joey with

his knife in hand.

"No, I'm not killing him. Whether he dies or not, they will still come looking. I'm not killing someone for no reason. Let's go."

They moved quickly down the corridor and up the stairs.

"Stay behind me," Frank said placing his hand back and hugging the wall as he ascended the steps. He slid the knife back into its sheath and pulled the handgun. At the top, he eased the door open and took a quick peek. There was no one there yet he could still hear the music blaring outside.

"Okay, let's move."

They navigated their way out and towards the back. As he retraced his steps he kept repeating the words to himself: *Stay calm.*

Closing in on the back door, they were seconds away from getting out when a guy with a goatee came into view. He was wearing a thin white shirt, and boxers, and carrying beer. He turned his head and locked onto Frank.

Frank went to raise his finger to tell him to stay quiet, when he dropped the beer and turned to flee. Before Frank could react, he had disappeared into the house and out of sight.

"Move it."

They burst forward entering the room the guy had been in, only to dart back out as he returned with a rifle in his hand. *No, no, no, this is not happening,* Frank told himself as he raised his own gun in defense and pushed Karla to the floor behind a chair. A sudden burst of bullets and the wall was peppered with holes. The guy pulled back behind a wall. Frank shuffled along trying to get closer. As the front of the barrel came into view around the corner of the wall, Frank grabbed it, shoved it up and it went off firing a hole in the ceiling. He lunged forward with his knee and pummeled the guy's stomach three times before headbutting his nose and sending him reeling back with his face covered in blood.

On the floor the guy started scrambling back trying to get away but Frank was on him faster than a fox on a rabbit. The guy let out a shout and Frank covered his mouth and forced his entire weight down on his thin frame. He was still jamming his gun into his gut and telling him to shut up when the man started wrestling with him. They twisted and turned, all the while he had the gun in one hand and the other hand was trying to keep the man from making any further noise.

He wasn't exactly sure how it happened but when the gun went off, his stomach sank. The look in the man's eyes went from fury to surprise, and then slowly his resistance weakened and the light in his eyes dimmed. There was no time to think, or have regrets, as he could already see two women further down the hall covering their mouths with their hands. It was like watching a train wreck occur in slow motion. As they removed their hands, their screams filled their air. Between the two of them, it was like hearing an air-raid siren.

Hauling himself up, now covered in the man's blood, he grabbed Karla's hand and they rushed the other way, ducked into a back room, and raced towards the rear sliding doors. Frank yanked on the door but it was locked. He flicked the locking mechanism up thinking it would unlock but it still didn't

"Stand back."

Frank took a few steps back and fired two rounds into the pane of glass. It shattered into thousands of pieces and they stepped through.

"Let's go!"

Karla clung to his hand as he led her out and they sprinted towards a thicket of trees. By this point he could hear people yelling and screaming "Intruder!" but they didn't slow down or stop to look back. They just kept running until they were hidden by the darkness of night and the trees that surrounded the property.

His mind was a whirlwind as they rushed through the thick underbrush and tried to put as much distance as possible between the house and themselves.

* * *

Butch heard the gunfire as he got closer to the house. He sped up and came soaring over a rise and headed straight for the house. Something wasn't right. His first thought as he saw the faces of those who had stayed back to keep watch over the women was that there had been an altercation or his dumbass cousins had been playing that game where they tossed a gun around with a live round inside.

He had visions of one of them writhing around on the floor with a bullet in his leg. He killed the engine on the ATV and hopped off without even letting the thing slow down. He rushed up to Tracey, one of his sisters, and grabbed her.

"What's going on?"

"Jimmy's dead."

"What?"

She pointed and was trying to get more words out but was in shock. Butch rushed into the house and was greeted by the sight of Jimmy's wife, Marilyn, hunched over him, screaming at the top of her voice.

"My baby, my baby. No!"

"Who did this?" Butch said. Her grief was so strong

she couldn't answer. "I said, who did this?"

"It was him, Butch," Joey said stumbling into view barely able to keep himself upright. He was massaging his neck which was red raw.

"What the fuck happened to you?"

"He jumped me."

"Who?" he yelled, getting annoyed at all the vague answers.

"Frank Talbot."

Butch backed up a little as though a heavy wave had just washed him out to sea.

"Talbot did this?" he muttered. Joey gripped the side of the doorframe to support himself and nodded affirmatively. His two sisters confirmed it. He gritted his teeth and squeezed his fists hard. Turning fast and heading back out the door, he rushed towards Gabriel and Tyrell and slammed his fist into Gabriel's jaw, knocking him to the ground. Next he pulled out his Sig Sauer and thrust it in the face of Tyrell.

"Where is he?" he yelled.

Tyrell tried to back up. "What the hell are you on about?"

Butch took a firm grip on the back of Tyrell's collar and began dragging him towards the house.

"Hey man, let go."

He stumbled a little and Butch told him to get up. He scrambled to his feet and they continued on until Butch threw him inside the house. Tyrell slid across the tiled floor like a rag doll. He was panting hard and looked scared.

Butch pointed a finger to Jimmy's body. "You see that!"

Tyrell just stared as Butch went over and scooped up some of the blood that had pooled around Jimmy's body and then he returned and wiped it across Tyrell's face and lips.

"Man, what the hell is going on?"

"I'll tell you what is going on." Butch brought up his gun and placed it against Tyrell's temple. "Now you have exactly one minute to tell me where Frank Talbot is or I will paint the wall behind you with your insides."

"I don't know a Frank Talbot."

"Fifty-two seconds."

Tyrell cowered back. "Look, man, I don't know what is going on here but I swear."

"Forty-seven seconds."

He could see Tyrell becoming more scared by the second but he was waiting to see it. The break. The look in their eye that all liars got when they had been found out.

"Thirty-four seconds."

Gabriel came into view a few feet away and he gazed at the body. "Listen, Butch, we have no idea who the hell you are on about."

"Twenty-one seconds."

Gabriel tried to intervene but he was pulled back by Bret. Butch observed them, looking for any indication that they might have known Frank. He figured they were being used as a distraction. It's what he would have done. It was smart but not smart enough. Or, perhaps he had got it wrong and he was about to end some random guy's life who happened to be in the wrong place at the wrong time. Either way he didn't care. All that mattered now was finding out how this had happened.

"Fourteen seconds."

Tyrell tossed his hands up. He was shaking uncontrollably. "Okay, man. We know Frank."

"Tyrell!" Gabriel shouted.

"No, fuck this. I'm not losing my life over some guy I barely know."

Butch pressed the barrel against his head even harder. "So talk."

"He told us to come over and check out what you had in place, you know, number of people, weapons, supplies because you didn't know us. But this..." Tyrell gazed at the lifeless body. "This was not what he said would happen. I would have never agreed to this if I knew he was going to kill someone."

Butch studied his face then lowered the weapon.

"And? Are there any others that came with you?"

"No, just us."

He narrowed his gaze.

"I swear," Tyrell replied.

"What about on Frank's island?"

"Um…"

"How many?" he bellowed.

Tyrell began counting with his fingers. "Five, eight if you include the kids."

Butch smiled then started laughing and walking ever so slowly back and forth looking out into the darkness of the night. "Eight if you include the kids. Oh, that is priceless." He then walked over to Joey and grabbed him by the head. "What happened to the twenty?" His eyes darted over to Dusty who was looking sheepish. "You fucking idiots. It was just Frank Talbot and there weren't twenty, were there?"

"There were two actually," Dusty said.

Keeping a hand on the side of Joey's neck, he turned to Dusty. "Shut up, you moron." He glared at both of them. "If you weren't my own blood I would put a bullet in both of you."

He slapped the side of Joey's neck a few times and then walked outside leaving them all wondering what he was about to do. Butch gazed around at the surrounding trees. He rested his weight back on one foot and nodded slowly.

"So you want to play games, Frank?" he shouted at the top of his voice.

There was no answer, just a chorus of crickets and tree frogs.

"Cause I can play games. I'm real good at games." He turned to Dusty and Joey and motioned for them to bring over the two guys.

"Listen up, take some of the cousins over to the island."

"Which one?"

He rolled his eye and slapped Joey across the face. "Which one do you think I'm talking about?"

"Right, Frank's, sorry, Butch."

"Exactly. Go over there, take Jackson, Palmer, Dusty,

and Bret and kill every last one of them."

"What?" Bret asked, shaking his head.

"You heard me."

He stepped back. "I'm not doing that."

Butch opened his eyes wide, unable to believe that his brother was speaking back to him. He walked over to him and grabbed him by the ear and twisted it hard. "If you live on this island you will do what you are fucking told, do I make myself clear?"

"It's murder, Butch, I'm not murdering anyone."

"Oh... You're not murdering anyone? Go take a fucking hard look at your cousin. And then tell me you aren't going to do anything!"

"I didn't say I wasn't going to do anything."

"No? Then why are you giving me grief? Huh? Do you expect me to negotiate? You want me to negotiate with someone that just killed one of our family?"

He shrugged. "No. I'm... I'm saying that this isn't right. There are other ways to handle this."

Butch rolled his lips between his teeth and stared deep

into his brother's eyes. He released him and walked over to Tyrell and placed the gun against his head.

"Frank! Listen up. I know you are out there."

He turned and told Jackson and Palmer to take Gabriel and go and put a hole in that boat. "If he thinks he's getting off this island he is mistaken."

Palmer shoved Gabriel forward. "Come on, dickhead, time to show us where this boat is."

Gabriel stumbled forward and landed on his knees. They grabbed the back of his collar and yanked him up. Butch then turned to Dusty and told him to take Ricky, Tyler, Ellis, Hudson, and Brooklyn over to the island. He turned towards his brother Bret, smirked, and then right in front of him told them exactly what he had said before. "Kill them all."

"And the kids?" Dusty asked.

"Ah… I was never fond of children."

Dusty nodded and took off to get the others.

Bret rushed forward towards Butch and grabbed a hold of him. "This is not right. You don't have to do this."

"It's already done, brother."

With that said he turned back towards the forest and continued to yell.

"I'm going to make this real easy for you, Frank. You have thirty minutes to come out unarmed and turn yourself over, otherwise I'm going to kill good ole Tyrell and then I'm going to kill Gabriel. You decide, Frank. Their lives or yours. It's up to you."

# Chapter 19

Jackson and Palmer took turns pushing Gabriel through the heavy woodland. They seemed to be finding enjoyment in seeing which one could make him stumble. Jackson looked to be close to two hundred and fifty pounds. He'd obviously eaten one too many chicken wings. His breathing was heavy and he kept stopping and leaning against a tree just to catch his breath. Palmer on the other hand looked as if he could have taken a page out of Jackson's diet book and gained a few pounds. His bony features protruded making him look like he'd been on a three-day drug bender. He kept clearing his throat like he had something stuck in the back of it. Both wore camouflage hunter's jackets, and work boots that looked like they had seen better days.

"How much farther is this boat?"

"Just beyond those trees," Gabriel said.

"You said that ten minutes ago."

"Well they all look the same."

Palmer gabbed a hold of him and pulled him in real close. "You better not be screwing us around."

"Why would I do that? You're the ones with the guns."

"That's right and don't forget it," Palmer said before shoving him forward with the butt of his gun. The truth was he was a little lost. When they had arrived, it had been close to the hall. With darkness shrouding everything and the leaves of the trees blocking out the moon's light, it was virtually impossible to determine where they were.

They continued on for another five minutes before Jackson's huffing and puffing got the better of him. He pulled out an asthma inhaler and took several puffs.

"I can't go any further. If I knew it was going to be this far I would have brought the ATV."

"Ah stop griping."

"Leave me here. You go with him and I'll wait here."

"No, he said we both had to go. I don't trust this asshole," Palmer said before glaring at Gabriel.

"Well then I need to rest a moment."

"You need to lose weight is what you need to do." Palmer tossed a broken stick into the forest and the sound of night critters scurrying could be heard along with the lapping of waves.

"Don't you guys get pissed off at him bossing you around?"

"Shut the hell up," Palmer replied

Jackson had one hand resting against a thick tree trunk and the other on his knee.

"I'm just saying…"

"Well don't."

"Okay, you good to go?" Palmer said to Jackson, all the while keeping his gun trained on Gabriel. He had contemplated making a run for it. He had a fifty-fifty chance they were going to kill him anyway but with Palmer's finger on the trigger he didn't think he would make it far.

Jackson reluctantly nodded.

They continued on, and after numerous questions and a hard jab from the gun to his gut, he told them that they had anchored not far from the hall. If he had to guess it was south. After another ten minutes of trudging through heavy foliage, they came out near the shoreline. It stretched before them, and water frothed against large boulders. A northeasterly wind blew against their faces as they made their way towards the boat that was moored to one of the many docks around the island.

"So tell me. Has Butch confiscated everyone's boats?"

It made sense that he would have claimed the one thing that others had stolen from the mainland. And of course, keeping all the boats together meant he could control the inhabitants of the island. The same people that looked so despondent at the meeting. Why were they not fighting back? Surely there was at least one family among the small amount that wasn't ready to put up with that jerk.

"That's none of your business."

"Seems a little odd that he would want to destroy a good boat, don't you think? Why not just bring it around to wherever he keeps his?"

Palmer jabbed Gabriel in the center of his back with his rifle. "If I have to tell you one more time to shut up, you are going to be spitting blood next."

"You got it, boss."

"What did you call me?"

"Boss."

He smirked. "That's right, bitch."

As they got closer to the boat that was bobbing around in the gentle waters, Gabriel remembered where Frank had stashed the rifles. He had covered them up with pine branches and a whole bunch of sticks about fifteen feet away from the dock.

When they reached the dock, Jackson was the first to head down to the boat.

"I really don't think you should destroy it," Gabriel said. "It's a waste."

Palmer smirked and pushed him up the dock behind Jackson. He had hoped he'd leave him at the edge of the island but this guy wasn't taking any chances.

"Now watch this," Palmer said as he raised his rifle and fired a round into the stern of the boat. Jackson did the same and as they were unleashing hell on the boat Gabriel knew that it was now or never. If he didn't take action, chances were he would be sinking to the bottom of the river along with that beautiful boat.

Palmer kept glancing at Gabriel while Jackson was hooting and hollering. Taking advantage of their momentary distraction, Gabriel charged at Palmer, knocking him off the dock into the water. He barely got a word out before he was coughing up water. Jackson was next; he knew that fat asshole wasn't going to be able to muster up enough energy to react in time. A sharp front kick to the stomach and he lost his balance and went in.

Moving at lightning speed, Gabriel sprinted up the dock, scrambled up the shore's incline, and made a beeline for the stash of rifles. All the while he could hear both of them cursing and water splashing around as they tried to get back on the dock. He knew he had only a matter of minutes before they would come after him.

He landed on his knees against the pile of pine branches, pulled them off, and scooped up a rifle. He covered the rest and readied himself for a firefight.

\* \* \*

Back at the Guthrie property, under the cover of darkness, Frank looked on in horror. This was the reason he hadn't killed Joey. If that other guy had just walked away, perhaps this whole plan wouldn't be coming apart at the seams. Both he and Karla were crouched down in the thick undergrowth staring out at Butch who had tied Tyrell to a post a few feet away from a fire pit. If it wasn't bad enough that he had the guilt of killing a man on his conscience, he now had the lives of two youngsters weighing down on him.

"What are you going to do?" Karla asked.

Frank stared blankly out at Butch and Dougie as they surveyed the area with at least another eight, maybe ten people. He recognized their faces. He'd seen them numerous times when he visited town. These were ordinary folk. Well, as ordinary as you could get for people obsessed with survival. Never in a million years could he have imagined that he would have killed one of the family, or that he would find himself in a life-or-death predicament.

"Do you really think he will kill that guy?" Karla asked. She was full of questions. Since they had vanished into the surrounding woodland, she wanted to know where he came from, how many others there were, were the police still in the town, and would he help them get off the island?

"I think he's capable of anything."

Frank got up and paced back and forth trying to get his head around this. He needed help, support from Sal and the others, but there was no time to head back to the boat. By the time he would have reached it, Tyrell would be dead.

"Shit!"

He pulled his phone out and wandered around trying to get a signal. One bar appeared and then it would vanish. "Oh come on," he muttered in frustration before putting it away and looking back out. He weighed the consequences of what might happen if he turned himself over. Would he really let Tyrell go? Where was Gabriel? His thoughts circled back around to his daughter, Sal, and the others. He'd made a big mistake in attempting to get back what was theirs. Then again, had they gone out and scavenged for more supplies, perhaps Butch would have shown up anyway. There was no clear way through this but he wasn't going to let Tyrell die, even if he had killed a cop in cold blood. He acted in the moment, just as he had with the man inside, except in that case it was an accident. They had struggled with the gun and it went off killing him. He didn't mean to kill him, he didn't want to kill anyone.

He had to think fast. Delay the inevitable. But how?

"Karla, listen. You said Butch took your husband's boat, right?"

She nodded.

"There is a boat nearby. I need you to do me a favor. I have an island not far from here. It's small. I will give you the GPS coordinates. If you can get over there, ask for a man named Sal. Tell him that I'm going to try and delay this but if things go bad, he is to look after Ella."

With that said he pulled out his anxiety meds and swallowed one down. With his face still masked up and goggles on, he told Karla to go. He told her to head towards the hall, go down to the water on the south side, and keep walking along until she saw the boat.

"But what about you?"

"Don't worry about me. Get your husband off this island, and anyone else who you know, but don't delay. Move fast. Go!"

She was transfixed on his face for a few seconds and then she thanked him again for getting her out and darted off into the night. Frank reached into his pocket and pulled out his flashlight. As much as he was willing to hand himself over, he wasn't just going to walk onto Butch's property without him releasing Tyrell, plus there was the glaring fact that as soon as he stepped out into the clearing, they would shoot him.

He breathed in deeply, calmed his mind, and focused on the task at hand.

"You can do this."

He squeezed his eyes shut then opened them and got up and walked towards the clearing. Once he made it to the edge he hollered to Butch.

"Butch. I'm ready to come out."

Butch darted out of the house and his eyes flitted around until he honed in on Frank's flashlight.

"But release Tyrell first."

"That's not how this works, Frank. You killed one of my kin."

"It was an accident."

"Oh, it was an accident. Well, that makes everything better. Dougie, it was an accident," he said in a mocking tone.

"Now listen up, fucker, you get your ass out here now or I'll kill him, and the other one, and then hunt you down. There is no way of getting off this island. So we can either do it the easy way or the hard way. What's it going to be?"

"I'm coming out. Don't shoot."

Frank stepped out into the clearing; he lowered his weapon on the ground as a sign that he wasn't looking for trouble. Not that it would help him but he was outnumbered and outgunned and he figured he could talk his way out of this if given the chance.

His eyes darted around looking for Butch's family members. He knew full well that Butch might have given them the order to shoot upon sight. As much as he wanted to go back and forth on this, he figured this was one negotiation he wasn't going to win. As he made his way across the clearing, more of Butch's family started to emerge. All of them were packing weapons and scowling at him like he was a piece of trash.

Right then a woman pushed her way through the others and fired a round at him. Fortunately it missed but it caused several of Butch's family to grab hold of her.

"You bastard!" she yelled. He figured it was the guy's wife.

"Take her inside," Butch said. He waited until they dragged her back inside the home crying and struggling before he continued on.

As he got closer, Butch nudged for Dougie and another one of his cousins to grab him. The moment they laid hands on him, he was thrown to the ground and had his hands tied behind his back. From the ground he looked up to see Butch walking over. He was about to say something when he felt the full force of a boot to the side of his face. That was followed by being flipped over and given a fierce beating. All the while Butch never said a word, he simply lashed out and laid into him with as much fury as he could summon. His hands were like fifty-pound weights hitting Frank in the face. When the beating was over, he rose to his feet and spat on Frank.

"Put him with the other."

Frank tried to force out words but his lip was busted up and blood was dribbling out of his mouth.

"You said…"

Again his words got a reaction out of him. Butch turned back and grabbed a hold of Frank's face by the cheeks with one hand. Dougie was holding him from behind, trying to keep him up. Butch squeezed hard and looked into his eyes.

"This kid is the least of your problems. I've sent my brothers and cousins over to your island to do what I should have done the first time."

Frank's eyes flared.

"Ah, there we go. That's the Frank I wanted to see. Get mad. There is nothing you can do about it. Tie him up, when the other one gets back we'll execute all three of them."

"Butch, we had an agreement," Frank yelled.

Butch didn't say another word. He disappeared inside the house while his family members looked on like some inbred hillbilly freaks that were ready to see an execution.

As Dougie tied rope around his chest and secured him tightly to a post about five feet away from Tyrell, Frank struggled to get loose. He needed to warn them. His hand went into his pocket to grab his phone, but Dougie saw him reach and he pulled it out, smiled, and then dropped it on the floor and crushed it below his boot.

"Oh, look at that. You're out of service."

"Listen, don't do this. I can fix this. I can…"

Dougie plowed a fist into his gut and he felt what little food he had eaten slide up into his throat.

"If I had my way, I would kill you right now."

"It was an accident."

Dougie stared at him and pulled a knife from his pocket and pushed up against his neck. "How about I slip, eh? It would be an accident."

# Chapter 20

Ella knew something wasn't right. She had gone out multiple times since her father had left to see if he'd returned but there was no sign of him. She lowered the night vision binoculars and headed up towards the house. Hayley was coming the other way looking perturbed.

"Has Gabriel texted you?"

"No."

"Do you mind me checking your phone?"

Ella took a few steps back and narrowed her eyes. "Excuse me?"

Hayley shifted from one foot to the next and had this look about her that made it obvious that she was in a salty mood.

"Look, I just want to check your phone."

As much as Ella was up for a good argument, she had bigger things to think about. She pulled it out and tossed it to her.

"Knock yourself out."

She brushed past her and made her way up to the house. She spotted Zach still patrolling one side of the island and Jameson was on the other. Sal was busy working on some contraption out in front of the house. A small oil lamp was hanging nearby to provide light.

"Sal. You heard from my father?"

He glanced down as he cut into a piece of wood, and shook his head. There was something in the way he looked at her that made her doubt his answer.

"He wouldn't be gone this long. Something's not right."

"Look, your father knows what he's doing. He'll be back."

"You mind me using your phone?"

"Where's yours?"

"Hayley is using it. She has trust issues."

"I think it's in the house and needs charging."

"Okay, whereabouts?"

Ella genuinely wanted to try texting her father. He had

been ignoring her texts and she wasn't getting anything back from Gabriel.

"Um, you might want to ask Gloria. I think she was using it last."

Ella gave a nod, and headed inside. Gloria had already settled the kids down for the night. When she found her, she was resting in a chair, reading a book.

"Hey Gloria."

She put her book down on her lap and looked up over her reading glasses.

"Hey, hon, you okay?"

"Did you see Sal's phone?"

"No."

"Oh. He said you used it."

"Not tonight. Who would I call?"

Ella bit down on her lip. It didn't take much to realize that he wasn't being truthful. She strolled back out and he had his back turned to her.

"What are you not telling me?"

"What?" he said spinning around looking a little

startled.

She put her hand out. "Phone. Come on."

"Ella, he didn't want to worry you."

"Oh really. Well, that failed. Come on, give it to me."

Sal sighed and fished around in his jacket pocket for the phone. She shook her head as she took it and checked the messages. Sure enough, there they were.

"He's not returning for twenty-four hours?"

"Now don't get panicked, that doesn't mean he has the virus."

"No it doesn't, but it sure as hell means he thinks he might have contracted it."

Ella tried to text him but there was no reply. She jumped down from the two steps that led up to the porch deck and started heading towards the boathouse.

"Ella, where are you going?"

"To find him."

"We don't have the boat, remember?"

She stopped in her tracks and balled her fists.

Sal put his hammer down and sat his ass cheek on the

white porch railing.

"Look, he's—"

Before the words came out of his mouth, Zach let out a loud cry.

"Boat coming. Boat coming!"

"What?" Ella spun around and rushed in the direction of Zach who was sprinting up to meet her. Ella assumed it was her father as who else would be visiting them at this hour. Sal leapt down from the porch with his rifle and once he caught up, Zach led them to the east side of the island. As they broke through the tree line and reached the shore, Ella lifted the night vision binoculars and then handed them off to Sal.

He took one look and went into panic mode.

"Jameson! Jameson!"

All of them turned and rushed up to find him. He was on the other end of the island already making his way up after hearing the commotion.

"What's going on?"

"We have company and they're armed."

Jameson rushed by them and bolted down to take a look for himself. By the time he had made it down there, they could see the boat without the use of binoculars.

"Make sure everyone has a firearm, and that there are no boats coming from any other direction. Zach, Sal, and I will make sure they don't get close to the island."

Ella rushed back up to the house. Out of breath and panting she burst through the rear door and told Gloria to get a gun.

"What is going on?"

She brought her up to speed before darting out the front door and called for Hayley who was perched on the edge of a boulder further down. She glanced back and cupped a hand around her ear as if she couldn't hear. There was a chance she couldn't as the thrashing of waves and the howl of the wind made it difficult.

Ella didn't wait to explain, she returned to the house, scooped up an AR-15, and headed over to the north side of the island. On a plot of land less than a few acres in size it didn't take long to get around the island. She gazed out using the binoculars. There was nothing. She scanned the horizon, it was all clear.

No sooner had she turned to head back than gunfire erupted. In all the time she had been at the police academy, nothing got her as anxious as the sound of a gun going off. It was much louder than they portrayed in the movies. The first time she had fired a live round, it shocked her. Eventually the more she fired, the less anxious she became. But that was in a safe environment, a firing range. This was the real deal. With a rifle strapped to her back and a Glock stuffed into the small of her back, she rushed back to where Sal and the others were. When she got there, she found them positioned in various places behind large boulders and thick tree trunks.

Zach was chuckling. "If these asshats thought they were going to creep up on us they must have been out of their mind. Who in the hell holds their rifles in their hands as they approach an island? Now had they been smart and laid them down in the boat, or chosen not to fire at us, they might have stood a chance of getting on here."

He turned and fired three times towards the boat that was pulling back.

"How many?"

"Looks to be about three."

Jameson shook his head. "Three people against us?"

Ella looked out and could see that one of them was rowing while the other two were now laying down in the boat with the barrels of their rifles perched on the edge. As they were getting farther away, they all heard another series of gunshots, however this time it was coming from the west side.

"Go," Jameson said. "We'll hold here."

Zach and Ella rushed up to the house. As they rounded the corner they saw a boat had landed on the west side. Three men were on the island. Ella's eyes flitted around for Hayley. She'd been down on the same side. Not wasting a second, Zach rushed up to the side of the house, crouched down by the corner, and started unloading rounds at them. They dispersed and took cover behind a cluster of trees. While he did that, Ella rushed into the house and found Hayley helping Gloria get the kids upstairs.

"Hayley," Ella was about to tell her to come with her when the windows on the house shattered with gunfire. The walls were peppered with holes. Ella dived towards Hayley and landed on her hard as drywall and pieces of wood spat all over the room. The curtains lifted up in the air as gusts of wind blew in and dust got in her mouth.

No sooner had it started than it stopped.

"Here take this." Ella gave Hayley the AR-15 and she crawled across the living room floor to the back of the door. "Oh, and give me my cell."

Hayley slid it across the floor to her. Ella shuffled over to the door where there was another rifle leaning against the wall in the corner. She snagged it up and stuck the barrel out the window, took a quick peek, and spotted one of the men making a run from one tree to the next. She fired four rounds and one of them hit, as he landed hard and let out a cry.

Hayley went over to the other side of the wall and placed her back to it. Ella waved her away.

"Get away from the wall."

She turned and saw several bullet holes.

"Where the hell am I meant to go?"

"Go up. Take the high ground. Perhaps you can spot them approaching."

"What do I do with this? I've never fired one."

She wanted to say, *are you kidding?* But unless she had grown up around guns she would have no clue. Hell, even Ella hadn't fired one until she got to the academy. It just wasn't something her father approved of. He had always kept his guns locked away and never once did he suggest going to the firing range. It was one of the reasons why he didn't want her becoming a cop, that and getting infected by someone with a cold.

She shook her head.

"Come over here."

Hayley scurried over holding the rifle like it was a bomb about to go off in her hand. She was probably better with a hairbrush or a blush applicator than a weapon.

"Pretty straightforward. Load and unload. Apply some pressure on this bolt catch here and pull back on the charging handle release. Then lock it back into place and rotate the weapon over and look down inside the chamber to make sure there is no ammo inside." She stopped to look out the window.

"Hold this a sec."

Ella pulled up her weapon and eased it out where a pane of glass had once been. She unloaded several rounds at a guy that was making his way around the side of the shore. He ducked down and then fired back a few rounds.

"Right, where were we?"

Hayley handed back the rifle. "With your left hand hit the top of the bolt catch and it sends the bolt forward back into place. Now grab a magazine and insert it into the magazine well then pull the charging handle back and release it. That's it. The rest is simple. Well, not simple but we don't have time for some long lesson."

No sooner had she said that than the house came under fire again by heavy rounds. Both of them hit the ground and she passed off the rifle to Hayley and motioned for her to head upstairs.

"Whatever you do, stay out of sight."

Hayley looked like she had already shit herself. She couldn't blame her. Ella hadn't felt this scared in her life. She shuffled across the ground and moved into a new position. Did they know how many were inside the house? She peered out and heard Zach call out.

"Ella, I've been hit!"

More gunfire erupted, however, this time it was coming from behind them which meant Sal and Jameson were coming under fire again. Ella moved quickly towards the back door while shouting up to Hayley to give her cover. Rounds snapped over her head as she circled the house and dived down close to where Zach was laying. He'd taken one in his right shoulder.

"Jameson!" she hollered but her voice was lost in the gunfire.

Though the injury didn't look life threatening, Zach was groaning in agony and clutching his shoulder. Blood trickled over his hand.

"I'm gonna get you fixed up, but you got to move."

She could see the fear in his eyes as he looked at her as if she was insane. One thing she had learned while in college was to stay calm. She couldn't forget the video they played for the entire academy of police dealing with a school shooting. They were running towards the school while kids were running out.

*"That's what you signed up for. When others are running away, you are going to be running towards danger."*

Cops in a small town could go their entire career only pulling their weapon a few times, whereas where she was going to be, in the heart of New York City, she would have had her hand on it daily.

Moving around the house, it was a miracle they didn't end up with a bullet in the leg or arm as the house was coming under heavy fire from every direction it seemed. As soon as they broke through the door and landed hard on the floor, Ella called for Gloria. She came down the stairs and Ella motioned to Zach and she didn't miss a beat. Whether she knew how to treat a gunshot wound was another thing but Ella didn't stick around to find out, she locked the back door and rushed to the front and did the same.

She hurried to one of the windows and stayed low looking out to see where they were. It was hard to see. Even though her eyes had adjusted to the dark, without floodlights or light from the moon hitting them, all she could make out was the occasional silhouette of someone darting in and out of trees.

"Hayley! You okay?"

"Of course I'm not."

From the kitchen she heard Zach speaking.

"Get me up, I'm going to help."

"You'll stay right where you are," Gloria muttered in her motherly tone.

Right then there was a beating on the back door and Ella saw Zach reaching for his gun on the ground.

"It's me. Let us in," Sal shouted.

Gloria got to the door before Ella could. As soon as it was open Sal came in holding Jameson who still appeared to have all his limbs intact.

Sal was breathing heavily. He immediately closed the blinds on the back windows and moved into position.

"Gloria. The kids?"

"They're safe. Upstairs."

Sal looked over to Ella. "You okay?"

"Just dandy," she replied in a mocking manner.

He turned out the lights and they all settled in for what they believed was going to be a long night. Though she felt a sense of relief flood over her, it wasn't over. Outside there were at least six armed and dangerous men preparing to unleash hell on them. And it wouldn't be over until either they were dead, or everyone inside the house was.

## Chapter 21

Shrouded by darkness, Gabriel stayed low to the ground. He had tried to put as much distance as possible between them and himself before they climbed out of the water but he could hear Palmer getting closer, hollering at the top of his voice.

"You made a big mistake, kid. When I get my hands on you…"

His mind was rushing a mile a minute. He feared for his life even though he was holding a rifle. When he shoved them into the water, he didn't have intentions of killing them. It was pure survival, a means of escape, that's all.

Gabriel positioned himself flat below a series of pine trees and covered himself with as much foliage as possible. Under the cover of night, it would have been hard to see him, at least that's what he hoped.

Keeping his finger close to the trigger, he waited and

watched as Palmer emerged from the shadows. He cast a glance around and trudged on shouting obscenities. Not that far behind him was Jackson.

"Hold up, Palmer."

"I told you we should have zip tied him."

"How was I to know?"

"You weren't, that's why you're an idiot."

When Jackson appeared in the clearing close to Gabriel, he was panting hard and struggling to get air into his lungs. His boots were only a few feet away from Gabriel's face, he could even smell the pungent stench of his body odor mixed with wet clothes.

"Palmer, let's just go back. We've done what he asked, we'll just tell him the kid escaped."

The sound of boots could be heard moving fast through the trees and then Palmer came into view. He grabbed a hold of Jackson and got real close to him.

"Escaped? Do you have any idea what he will do to us if we allowed that kid to escape?"

"Then we tell him that we had to shoot him, and his

body fell into the river."

Palmer released his grip and Jackson smoothed out his wrinkled clothing.

"Fuck! This is so messed up. Alright let's go, but if he can tell that we're lying, I'm telling him you let him escape."

"Oh come on, Palmer, I wasn't the first one he knocked in."

"Maybe not, but you didn't do anything."

They began walking off.

"How could I? The kid was like a jackrabbit. I've never seen anyone move that fast."

"No, you've just never moved fast yourself."

"Really? You want to go there?"

Their voices became faint as they strolled off into the darkness and eventually disappeared out of sight. Gabriel breathed out hard and remained in that spot for what felt like at least another thirty minutes before he edged his way out and brushed all the pine needles off his clothes.

The first thing he did was dig into his pocket for his

cell phone and try to warn Ella and the others about the men coming to the island. What he didn't realize was that it was already too late.

* * *

Tyrell gazed despondently at the ground when Frank looked over at him.

"Tyrell, you okay?"

He cast a sideways glance. "I'm sorry, Frank. He had a gun to my head."

"I probably would have done the same." Frank tried again to get his arms free but it was useless. They had tied the restraints so tight it was nearly cutting off the circulation in his arms. He surveyed the area, and winced as he heard distant gunfire. It was barely audible but he knew it was coming from his island. The thought of them massacring the others sent him in a cycle of anger, frustration, despair, and then back to being hopeful that he could get out before it was too late. He gazed into the fire pit and watched the flames flicker, and listened to the sound of wood popping. An overwhelming sense that he was out of control and a wave of regret for stepping foot on the island hit him.

Fifteen minutes passed, maybe more before Palmer and Jackson reappeared. Frank's brow knit together as he noticed that Gabriel wasn't with them. They glanced over at Frank before making their way towards the house. They hadn't got within ten feet when Butch came out and burst into a rant.

"So where is he?"

"Uh, dead. He tried to escape and well... his body is in the river," Palmer said.

Butch, who was probably used to them lying, looked at Jackson. "Is that right?"

He nodded affirmatively like a young child who was hoping to escape the wrath of an angry parent. He shook his head and looked at them as if he wasn't sure whether to believe them.

"Well I guess that just speeds things up," he said before walking past them and making his way over to Frank and Tyrell.

"Seems your friend took the easy way out."

"Bastard," Tyrell said.

Butch scowled and then threw a right hook. "None of this would have happened if you had just stayed on your island."

"Oh, it's our fault?" Frank said. "I think you must be suffering from a slight case of amnesia. You stole my supplies."

"And I would have gladly given them back, under certain conditions."

"They weren't yours to make conditions on."

He laughed and pulled out a cigarette. "Now I've been thinking what would be a suitable death for both of you."

He pulled out his handgun and placed it against Frank's head. "A bullet to the head? Would be quick, practically painless. It would almost be like I was extending mercy to you. No, then I thought about infecting you. I mean, I hear that is one hell of a way to die. Hours of excruciating pain, it seems fitting for someone like you."

"You've made the assumption I wanted to kill him. Think about it, Butch. If I wanted to kill, I would have killed Joey. I could have done it but I didn't. I cuffed him instead. Hell, I even could have shot your cousin before he went for his gun but I didn't. What happened to Jimmy has happened, and I'm truly sorry. But it was an accident."

"Sorry? Like you are about Clarence? Was the round in his head an accident?"

Frank frowned as he thought back. "Clarence? I never shot Clarence. That was that lunatic Abner Rooney, and your brother finished him off. I just happened to be there."

"Accidents, coincidences, I got to say, Frank, you do have a way of getting yourself in the wrong place at the wrong time." He tapped him on the side of the face. "But you raise an interesting point. What were you doing there?"

Frank gazed down at the ground and that's when the idea came to him.

"The same reason your guys were there. Guns, and a shitload of ammo."

Butch stepped back, regarding him with an expression of skepticism.

"They told me there were none."

"None they could see. Abner might have been a lunatic but he was smart and made sure those weapons were not easy to find."

"Well, thanks for the heads-up, I'll have some of my men tear the place apart."

Frank sniffed hard and shook his head. "You won't find them. And believe me there are a lot. Enough I would say to arm all your family, the people on this island, and then some. More than enough ammo to last you at least one or two years."

"So where are they stored?"

"I'll take you to them."

"No, you will tell me where they are."

"Hard to explain really. Better you take me over there."

Butch got real close and stared at him. Frank startled chuckling.

"You got trust issues, Butch?"

After he said that, Butch pulled out a serrated hunting knife and went over to Tyrell and jammed it against the side of his neck. Tyrell let out a cry.

"I'm not screwing around. Where are they!"

"Don't tell him, Tyrell, he's only going to kill us anyway, isn't that right, Butch?"

Tyrell let out a gasping noise as Butch applied pressure.

"Alright, alright, I'll tell you. Just ease up."

"Fuck man, don't you ever know when to close your mouth?" Frank said.

"Screw you, Frank. You got us into this. I'm not dying for you."

Before he could say anything, Dougie came out of the house, yelling for Butch.

"Butch, you need to take this."

He sneered at both of them, then released the knife

and charged away. Frank watched as he went into the house. As soon as he was gone he turned to Tyrell.

"Listen up. You want to get out of here, you are going to have to do everything I say."

"Forget it. I'm done listening to you. Hell, you are as mad as your daughter said."

Hearing that was like a knife going through his heart. It wasn't as if he expected her to think that he didn't have issues. He did. But he'd improved, at least Sal thought so.

"Tyrell. I'm serious. You want to live, you are going to need to run with me on this."

Tyrell sighed, then nodded. Frank began to explain what he wanted him to tell Butch. It was a fifty-fifty chance that it would go wrong but those odds were better than the ones they had right now. The fact was Tyrell wasn't even there on the day they visited Abner's place. He knew about the table but not how it operated. That was his ticket out otherwise he might have taken Tyrell and killed Frank.

When Butch came out of the house about five minutes

later, his face was a beet red, and he looked as if he was about to explode. He yanked his knife from the sheath on his leg and rushed up to Tyrell and placed it against his neck.

"You better have something good to tell me."

Tyrell gulped. "All I know is it's below the pool table."

"Thank you, then I don't need you." He tensed up as if he was about to slash Tyrell's neck when Frank spoke.

"You don't want to do that," Frank blurted out.

"Why not? Seems your people have shot one of mine."

"Self-defense. You act aggressively, what the hell do you expect people are going to do? Listen, Tyrell's right. It's below the pool table but unless you have some drilling device you aren't getting through fifteen feet of concrete and steel without my help."

"What do you mean?"

"I know how to operate the mechanism that brings it down. I saw him do it."

Butch pulled his knife away from Tyrell and walked towards Frank.

"So how's it work?"

"Like I said. It's not easily explained. There are sensors that are weight sensitive. They aren't marked out. Unless you know where to stand, it doesn't matter what button you press, you aren't getting in."

Butch looked away and gnawed on the inside of his cheek.

"Okay. You are going but he doesn't need to go."

"You kill him, you can forget getting inside."

Butch narrowed his eyes and paced back and forth for a few seconds twisting the knife around in his hand.

"And what do you get out of this?" Butch asked.

Frank sighed. He hesitated before he spoke. "I know you're not going to let me live, but all I ask is that you leave the others alone. They haven't done anything to warrant this. You want someone to blame. Blame me. But leave them out of this."

Butch smirked and then chuckled wiping his brow with the back of his hand. "You know, Frank, you're a real humanitarian. Are you really willing to die for others?"

"If it means they get to live, yeah. But you have to promise to be true to your word."

"You got trust issues, Frank?" he said throwing back the same words Frank had said.

"So? Is it a deal?" Frank asked.

He chuckled and shook his head. "Yeah, it's a deal. I would shake on it but you're kind of tied up," he said before walking away.

"So when do you want to go?"

With his back to them he replied, "Soon, Frank. Soon. I just need to give the boys the heads-up."

He wandered off and disappeared into his home. Tyrell turned to Frank. "You trust him?"

"Of course not, he's going to screw us over the first chance he gets. I expect that."

"Why do I get a sense you're not telling me everything?" Tyrell asked.

"Cause a gambler always keeps his cards close to his chest."

* * *

Not far from Butch's property, Gabriel was completely lost. After walking for what seemed like an hour, he eventually emerged near a property that didn't look anything like the one he'd been at. With it still being night he couldn't tell if he had gone east or west. He looked up at the stars and moon and tried to remember what his old teacher had said about being able to navigate by way of the stars. He must have blocked it out as he had no idea now.

He was about to head up to the house when his phone buzzed. Fishing it out, he saw a text from Ella. He'd managed to get through to her earlier but they had come under heavy fire and so she'd told him she'd get back to him as soon as there was a clear moment.

"Is my father alive?"

"The last time I saw him he was. I don't know right now. Hell, I don't even know where I am on this damn island." He looked around for a sign, some indication of where he was but there was nothing. It was nothing but woodland, trails, and flat land. He continued up towards the house. The lights were on, he just hoped they weren't Butch's family.

*"Zach has been shot. He's alive but in a lot of pain."*

*"Shit."*

*"If you see my father, let him know I love him. I don't know if we are getting out of this."*

*"Don't say shit like that."*

*"I'm scared, Gabriel."*

*"I know, just hang in there. Is Hayley okay?"*

*"Yeah."*

*"Listen, we'll come to help, trust me. We're coming."*

*"Hurry."*

And that was it. He sent another text message but didn't get a reply. He felt like an idiot for promising her something when he had no clue where the hell he was. He looked up and pressed on towards the house. When he climbed onto the porch and peeked in through the window, he saw a family huddled together in a living room. They looked to be discussing something. A large kitchen knife rested on the table and a baseball bat was leaning up against the counter. He couldn't make out what they were saying but the conversation with a dark-haired man looked to be heated. He contemplated just pressing on into the darkness of the night but he was done running. Something had to be done. This was bigger than his fear.

He moved towards the door, readied the gun, and turned the knob.

If they were dangerous, he was about to find out.

# Chapter 22

Chaos erupted as Gabriel rushed into the house. The dark-haired man rose from the table, grabbing the baseball bat. Not that it would have been much use against a gun but he certainly looked as if he wasn't prepared to go down without a fight. He swung it back and forth shouting for him to get out of the house.

He pushed the woman and two kids behind his back and stared at Gabriel.

"Are you here to kill us? Did Butch send you?" the man asked.

Gabriel shook his head. "No I thought you might be working with him."

Confusion spread across their faces, as it did his.

"Why the hell would I work for that controlling asshole?"

"So you're not family?"

His eyes widened. "Hell no."

Gabriel lowered his rifle. "I'm Gabriel, and you are?"

Still clutching the baseball tightly he muttered, "Landon and this is my wife, Sandra."

His two kids peered out from behind him, a look of shock on their faces.

"I'm sorry to barge in this way. I wasn't sure if you were part of his family."

"Where are you from?"

"It's a long story. Queens, but I came here with a friend of mine, Ella Talbot."

"Frank Talbot's daughter?"

He nodded. "You know him?"

"Who doesn't?" He released his death grip on the bat. "I'm a doctor in Clayton and besides him always walking around with a face mask on, which I have to say now was a smart thing to do, he would always be coming into the office expressing that he had some new disease. I think I've seen him more than any patient in the town."

"Butch has a friend of mine, I'm pretty sure he plans to kill him along with those on Frank's island. And while

I didn't hear him, I think he has Frank now."

Landon looked at his wife. "I told you. He's out of control." He looked back at Gabriel. "Look, I would like to help but there's just a few of us islanders. We're a tight-knit community but no way prepared to take on these guys."

"So what's the baseball bat and knife for?"

He cast a glance at the items. "Protection."

"Be honest with him, Landon," Sandra said. Landon looked at her with hard features. The tension in his face softened and he sighed. "I was going to speak with the others on the island, see what we could do about him. I know there aren't many families here right now but there's enough men to deal with him."

Gabriel smirked. "Vigilante style. I like it."

"Ah, well, I was thinking that until my wife here was trying to talk me out of it."

"I don't want you getting hurt."

Gabriel took a seat at the table. The chair screeched as he pulled it out. "Look, whatever he is doing here, it's going to get a lot worse. One of his cousins was killed and now he thinks he's going to get justice by killing Frank, Sal, and my friends. I need to stop him but I can't do it alone. Do you have a boat?"

Landon ran a hand through his hair and leaned against the kitchen counter. "Had. I had one. He took it, like he did most of our supplies."

Gabriel narrowed his eyes. "Why didn't you leave the first chance you got?"

"And go where? Clayton is a mess, the whole country is and without supplies…" he trailed off.

"Better to stick with the devil you know than the devil you don't. I gotcha," Gabriel replied.

Sandra went over to the stove and returned with some tea. "You want a hot drink?"

"Thank you but I have to go. For all I know Frank and Tyrell are dead but I need to see."

Gabriel stood up. "You don't have any guns?"

"No. But I'm pretty sure Tom Hannigan has one. He said that he had his locked up in the basement behind a pile of boxes."

"Right, but I mean you?"

"I was never a firearms owner."

"I can get you one, show you how to use it, that is if you still want to help?"

"We would need the others."

Gabriel walked over to the door. "Well?"

Landon looked at Sandra and her eyes dropped.

"Keep the kids safe," he said leaning forward and giving her a peck on the forehead. They left the residence and Gabriel got directions back to the south side of the island from him. Upon returning to the spot where they stashed their rifles, he handed one to Landon and took him through the basics of using it. After he slung the other one over his shoulder, they pressed on towards Tom Hannigan's house.

A strong breeze blew through the trees kicking up dust and making the night seem darker.

"How many others do you think will help?"

"There are ten families on the island, possibly seven of

them might help, maybe more, maybe less."

"It will have to do."

\* \* \*

Frank felt blood rush back into his limbs as they cut free his restraints. Butch was preparing to leave for the mainland so the place was a hive of activity.

"What about Tyrell?"

"Like I said, he stays here. And if for even a second you try to screw me over, I'll make a call and my brother will kill him. You understand?"

Frank nodded while rubbing his red wrists. His arms ached from where they'd been  wrapped so tight.

"Dawson, Adam, Randall. You're coming with me."

Butch glared at Frank. For someone who exercised his authority over others, he certainly wasn't taking any chances. Since Frank had been tied to the post he'd watched different members of Butch's personal and extended family come and go. He knew that six of them had gone to his island, three of them were going with Butch, and there were Dougie, Bret, Palmer, and Jackson staying behind with the women. Jimmy was dead. He figured that at best there were about eighteen of them. Thirteen guys and five women. Nine staying behind. If this worked, and Sal and the others took out the ones attacking the island, it would mean only dealing with nine people, he thought. Those were better odds.

Butch leered at him. Right now he had to focus on these four.

"Okay, get on the ATV and head down to the dock. I want to get this done before midnight." He then turned to Dougie. "Wait on my call."

"You got it, brother," he said with a devilish glint in his eye.

The journey down to the boats was bumpy. The reflection of the moon on the water caught his eye as they zipped down thin trails in between the trees. The engines growled violently. They had him handcuffed around Dawson's waist. To look at them anyone would have thought they were just typical, run-of-the-mill blue-collar workers. Nothing would indicate they were capable of this. And yet it didn't seem like a far stretch of the imagination. With no law around to stop them, and no one with enough balls to stand up to them, it was just a matter of time before someone would try to dominate others. It just so happened to be Butch.

* * *

When they arrived at Tom Hannigan's house, his family had turned in for the night. Landon banged on the door for several minutes before the lights came on in the house and a bleary-eyed guy, who couldn't have weighed more than a hundred and forty pounds, came to the door in a dressing gown. He adjusted his spectacles and squinted as he opened the door, then pushed wide the storm door.

"Landon?"

"We need to speak."

"Come in."

Inside it smelled like lemon. As they entered the hallway of a beautiful house that had hardwood floors, granite countertops, and a chandelier hanging from the ceiling, a woman appeared at the top of the stairs.

"Tom, who is it?"

"Just Landon. Go back to bed."

With that said, he waved them into the spacious kitchen with a cathedral ceiling. The entire residence was made from logs. A large painting with a portrait of his family hung above a fireplace in an area that served as the dining room. He beckoned them on into a study and closed the French doors behind him.

All around the room were shelves of old leather books, some of them had brass buckles on them. It looked as if he had collected every ancient book known to man.

Tom leaned against his desk looking like a Wall Street executive.

"What's going on? Who is this?" He glanced at Gabriel.

"This is Gabriel." He never expanded upon that but stayed on topic. "That conversation we had after the meeting. You still want to go through with it?"

He smoothed a hand over his black hair and got a dead

serious look on his face.

"Does Sandra know?"

"I told her this evening," Landon said.

"And?"

"She's not for it, but she's not against it. Listen, you know as well as I do that this isn't going to work. The guy is a lunatic. Would you have put up with this before the virus?" Before Tom could answer, Landon answered for him. "No. Neither would I, that's why we need to do something about it."

"I don't know, Landon. It seems a bit sudden."

"You told Maria, didn't you?"

He nodded sheepishly.

"She doesn't want any harm coming to the kids."

"It's going to happen one way or another, Tom. Tell him, Gabriel."

Gabriel took a deep breath and began to relay what had happened starting with Butch taking Frank's supplies, and then the death of his cousin and how he'd sent men over to kill his friends on the island.

"I understand but let's face it. Do you blame him?"

Landon put a hand on his hip and leaned in to him. "Are you kidding? It doesn't matter who's to blame here. Retaliation is a sign of the future. What happens if one of us steps out of line, or looks at him the wrong way? Eh? What then?"

Tom sniffed and rubbed sleep dust from his eyes. "Well it won't happen."

Landon spun around and ran a hand around his neck. "Oh come on, Tom, don't be so damn gullible. Men like Butch don't use diplomacy, they rule with an iron fist. And no matter how you try and spin this, or suck down what he's telling us, he is attempting to rule over us. And I for one am not going to sit by while my family gets the shit end of the stick and he gets to thrive in the lap of luxury."

"But he's going to protect us."

"Is that Maria speaking or you? Do you honestly believe that?"

"Well…"

"Don't even answer it. I could have blown you away with a rifle the moment you opened the door. Where are his men patrolling your house? My house or any of ours? He's looking out for number one, and that's it. All the rest is lip service."

Gabriel leaned back against a desk and just let Landon do all the talking. He was obviously so riled up that he didn't need his input.

"I don't know, Landon."

"Tom, how many years have you and I been coming here?"

He scratched the side of his face and looked off into the distance. "Twenty-six."

"How many years has he been here?"

"Not long. He only comes here for his retreats."

"Exactly. This isn't his damn island. It's ours. It's time we take it back."

Tom nodded ever so slightly. Though he didn't look confident or completely in agreement, he looked open to ideas. "So, how are we going to do this?"

Gabriel pushed off the desk and stepped forward. "That's where I can help."

\* \* \*

Bullets shattered all the lower windows and glass spat in every direction. Sal had pulled them back into the center of the house and away from the walls that were being drilled with rounds. His adrenaline had kicked into gear as they returned fire.

"How the hell are we going to get out of this?"

"How the hell should I know?" Jameson said before looking over to Zach. "How's he doing?"

Gloria had done her best job of patching Zach up but he didn't look well. His skin had gone a pasty white and he was rolling around in pain. "Gloria, there is some rye whiskey in the cupboard in the basement."

Jameson looked at Sal with an expression of amusement. "You looking to get drunk before you die?"

"It's not for me, it's for Zach. At least it might take the edge off."

"Old style, I like it."

Outside it went quiet. It was hard to make out where the men were and they didn't want to get too close to the windows out of fear of being shot in the face. Jameson had come within inches of having his ear torn apart the last time he looked out.

"Sal, you might want to come and see this," Ella shouted out. Staying in a crouched position he shuffled across the floor and up the stairs. When he made it to the top, Ella was positioned behind a thick mahogany dresser drawer. She had placed it front of the windows.

"Smart idea."

"It lets me look out without them seeing me," she said peering through a thin section on the far right side.

"What do you want?"

She motioned with her finger towards a section of the property. There was a light flickering. Like a large flaming torch.

"I think they are going to burn us out."

"Holy shit."

He backed up fast and rushed down the stairs.

"Jameson, come with me," he said heading towards the basement.

"But…"

"Just come. Ella, take over down here. Whatever you do, don't let them through those doors. And one last thing. When I tell you to start shooting, unleash hell on them."

Sal pressed on down the steps and headed over to the metal storm doors. He started unlocking two large locks.

"Um, what the hell are you doing?"

"We're going out."

Jameson lunged forward and slammed his hand against the lock. "Are you out of your mind? There are six guys out there. We have a wounded guy inside, plus three women and three kids. You want to leave them here to defend themselves?"

"We don't have any choice. They are going to burn us out. They are watching the windows. Ella is going to cause a distraction, and lay down enough firepower that we can make a break for the cluster of trees close by."

"And if we don't make it?"

"Then I guess it's been a pleasure."

"You have been around Frank way too long."

The corner of Sal's lip curled up. Once he got the second lock off, he took a deep breath and then shouted out to Ella.

"Let it rip, Ella."

Right then multiple rounds erupted on the north side of the house. There were too many for it to have been just Ella and Hayley.

"You ready?"

"No."

"Good."

With that said he flung the door open and they ascended the five steps up to the east side of the house. With all the shooting going on, it was hard to tell if they were firing at them or Ella. As soon as they were out, he slammed the door closed and locked it while Jameson kept his eyes peeled for threats.

Once the door was locked, the silhouette of their two

shadows burst out across the grass and into the tree line.

## Chapter 23

Upon arriving on the mainland, Frank's anxiety was at an all-time high. He knew that if anything went wrong, it was lights-out for them all. All the way there, Butch had been droning on about how he was changing the hearts and minds of those living on the island. The guy was crazy. He actually thought he was doing good by them.

When they made it to Abner Rooney's place, Butch had Dawson hold Frank while Adam and Randall went inside to make sure there were no threats. While they were looking around they all took in the sight of his ramshackle abode. It had been peppered with bullet holes and all the windows were shattered.

"So why did you kill him, Frank?"

"Who?"

"Clarence."

"Didn't you hear anything I told you?"

"I did but nothing but lies have come out of your

mouth since this whole thing has kicked off."

"Believe what you want. I didn't kill anyone."

"Not even Jimmy?"

"The gun went off as we were struggling."

"But somebody had to pull the trigger."

Adam and Randall reemerged and gave them the all-clear signal.

Butch motioned with his hand. "Alright, Frank, lead the way."

Dawson shoved him forward and they ambled up to a door that was barely hanging from its hinges. Glass crunched beneath their boots as they entered the final resting place of Abner Rooney. The smell of death stung Frank's nostrils. In the heat of the summer it hadn't taken long for the bodies to begin to rot. Frank noticed that Joey and the others had torn the place apart searching for the weapons, but to no avail.

"I've got to say, Frank. It takes either a brave or a stupid man to turn himself in on behalf of his friends. I have to admit, we could have used a man like yourself."

"I don't work well with others."

Butch scoffed. "Explains a lot."

They entered the room that contained the pool table. Butch gazed around and looked intrigued by the place.

"Those lazy bastards didn't take the booze. Adam, Randall, go grab up some of those bottles. We'll take that with us. Tonight we celebrate."

He looked like a kid on Christmas morning, and then when he caught Frank staring, he went over and shoved him towards the table. "Get it working."

"Alright. Calm down."

Frank went to the far end. The last time he'd been this nervous was when he visited the doctor's office. He hated the place. It was like a germ magnet.

"So, you are going to need to stand in certain places around the table."

Butch scowled. "Why?"

"Like I said. It works using pressure plates and sensors. So Butch, if you want to go to the other side, and have Dawson on the left and maybe Adam on the right, we'll get this show on the road."

"Randall, get over here. You can take my spot."

"Is there a problem?" Frank asked.

Butch didn't answer him. He simply squinted and pushed Randall into his spot.

"You need to get a little closer." Frank went around and adjusted them so they were practically touching the table itself. He then returned to his spot. As he looked around at them he saw Butch place a hand against his side holster. He didn't trust him. That was going to be a problem. Frank contemplated whether to do what he had in mind. Hell, he wasn't even sure if it was going to work a second time but he had nothing to lose. The second they had those guns he'd be a dead man. That was for sure. And as for Ella, Sal, and the rest of them, they would also be dead. Butch wasn't a man of his word. He was a man of vengeance.

Frank breathed in deeply. As much as he didn't want to do this, he knew he had to.

Butch tossed his hands up in the air. "Come on,

Frank, let's get this going."

Frank acted as though he was trying to find the exact spot to stand on. He gazed over at Butch. His hand was twitching on that gun, just waiting to pull it. Frank slipped his hand beneath the pool table. His fingers ran over the smooth wood, searching for the two buttons.

"Ready?" Frank asked. When he asked, all he wanted to see was which of them he could grab a gun from.

His finger trembled as it touched the left button. He pushed it in and what happened next was beyond anything he had ever seen. Flames burst out the sides and the far end of the table turned a fiery blue and red, like an incinerator being switched on. Shock, disbelief, and agony spread on the faces of Randall, Adam, and Dawson as their bodies were engulfed in flames.

They stumbled back, dropped their weapons and Randall fell to the floor rolling around in agony, trying to put himself out. Butch pulled his gun but in the chaos erupting around him, he couldn't see Frank.

He fired a round off, but Frank was already gone.

Without a second to lose, Frank had shot towards Adam, snagged up his AK47, and ducked out of the room. Gasping for air as smoke poured out of the room he double-timed it down the corridor heading for the back door only to have multiple rounds fired at him. He spun and fired back, then realized Butch wasn't there. He had just unloaded at the wall hoping to hit him in mid-sprint.

Frank kicked the rear door open and bolted out as he heard Butch scream his name. The sound of his boots behind him made him rush for the nearest place of cover. He ducked down behind an old fishing boat and crept around to the far end so he could get a better view of Butch. He fully expected him to come bursting out and when he did he would unleash a flurry of rounds and end him.

Seconds, then minutes passed and when he still hadn't emerged, Frank moved into another position thinking he might have come out the front entrance. Still nothing. Smoke was beginning to pour out of the west end of the building and for a moment he thought that perhaps he'd got stuck. Possibly he'd succumbed to the smoke. But that idea was quenched when he shot out the front end, rushing for the truck. He was coughing up a storm and his face was black with smoke. As he ran he unloaded a wide spread of bullets to cover himself but it wasn't going to be much use. Laid out on the ground, Frank squinted with one eye and fired twice. As if he'd tripped over a line, Butch collapsed on the ground. He hit the gravel hard and let out a bloodcurdling scream.

As Frank got up to head over to him, Randall came out of the door and started firing at him.

"What the fuck?" Frank said as he hit the ground and rolled out of view. Randall's skin was burnt down one side and most of his clothes were gone. How the hell he was managing to stand or shoot for that matter was beyond Frank. Frank hurried to the far end of the boat he was behind and climbed up and over. Randall was gasping for air and dragging his right leg as he headed towards the boat.

Frank's eyes darted to Butch who had crawled away from where he'd fallen. It didn't take much to take out Randall. He fired multiple times and the burnt excuse for a man fell to the ground writhing in agony. One more shot and there was silence.

"Frank, I got to admit, that was some smart thinking but a sloppy decision. Did you really think that I wasn't expecting you to try something?"

Frank could hear his voice but couldn't tell where it was coming from. A hard wind blew in and with the sound of the river behind it, it was hard to pinpoint his location.

"That black boy is as good as dead. Whatever happens now, you only have yourself to blame."

\* \* \*

Gabriel, with the help of Landon and Tom had managed to gather together another four men from the island, willing to take control of the situation. They had been waiting in a heavy thicket of trees, looking for an opportunity to move in on the property. Men and women moved back and forth between the house and fire pit.

"Dougie. Phone call. It's Butch," a blond female called out from the house.

Dougie had been sitting by a large fire along with the other three drinking beers and roasting what looked like chicken or marshmallows on a stick.

"So listen up, the only way this is going to work is we move in fast. The focus is to get Tyrell out safely, that's it."

"That might be it for you. But not for me," Landon said. "Those fuckers hit my wife when they came to our house and took what we had."

"Whatever. The rest of you fan out and keep your weapons on those around the camp, two of you break off and head for the house."

"And if they go for their weapons?"

Gabriel didn't hesitate to reply. "Do I even need to answer that?"

Only four out of the six had weapons. Gabriel had given one to Landon, and Tom had one, and Pete

Rolands had the other. The other two were carrying baseball bats.

"I don't know about this," Tom said.

"Look, we have the element of surprise. But if you are having second thoughts, now is the time to say because once we're out in the clearing there is no going back."

"So when do you want to go?"

Gabriel looked back towards the campfire. Palmer kept tossing some food at Tyrell and making jokes about how they were going to roast him over the fire like a pig, the first chance they got. Gabriel was about to answer that when Dougie came charging out of the house.

"Looks like your time is up," he said pulling his handgun from his side.

"Now!" Gabriel said.

Like a stealth army unit, they moved out from the shadows of the forest into the clearing.

"Get down now," Gabriel shouted with his gun towards Dougie. Anyone who had an ounce of brains would have dropped their weapon. Not that idiot. He spun around and Gabriel didn't even hesitate, he squeezed the trigger and spat out several rounds taking him down. Palmer and Jackson went for their guns and retreated back while firing off rounds, and Palmer hit the ground as Landon opened fire on him. Jackson knew he was shit out of luck and tossed his weapon. Unfortunately, he took one in the arm before he could throw his arms up. He writhed around on the ground like a beached whale before Landon put him out of his misery. The only one that hit the ground with his hands out was Bret.

"Don't shoot him," Gabriel said trying to get the others to stay calm in a stressful situation. He motioned for the others to go check the house for the women. A couple had already come out and had dropped to their knees.

\* \* \*

Frank crept along from one boat to the next, trying to figure out where he was. He spotted the truck but he wasn't in it or even under it.

"Now listen up, if you want your daughter and the others to live then you better pay attention." He knew he'd hit Butch badly as there was an edge of desperation to his voice that he hadn't heard before.

Frank ducked down and listened intently. Wind was kicking up dust and making it hard to see. He coughed into his face mask and adjusted his position.

"You let me go, they live and I'll call my men off. You shoot me, and they will kill your family. Do I make myself clear?"

Frank scoffed. After all the talks this guy had given on being a survivalist. The way he portrayed himself as a bad ass who was not to be fucked with. Here he was negotiating for his life. It was all an act.

A huge gust of wind blew in and a tarp went up in the air, and Frank heard him cough. Moving quickly across the yard, he ducked behind a boat and slowly crept around it until he stepped out and found Butch lying against the side of the boat gripping a bloody leg. He immediately reacted by lifting his gun but Frank just shook his head.

"You'll be dead before you squeeze."

Butch got this scared look on his face. He was showing a different side that he'd hidden from the others, the one that was scared to die. The one that realized this could have all been avoided if he hadn't been an asshole and taken all the supplies.

"Your call, Frank. But if they don't hear from me, they are going to be cooked alive."

"You are one sick fuck."

"Sick fuck? I wasn't the first one to pull the trigger. So I took some of your supplies, don't tell me you wouldn't have done the same thing."

"But you didn't need it. I saw what you had. You had more than enough."

Butch scoffed and looked down, bringing his rifle to the side.

"You think I can have a cigarette before you do it?"

Frank stared at him blankly with his finger twitching near the trigger.

"Go ahead."

He chuckled a little and coughed as he pulled out a pack of cigarettes. Both rounds had gone in his thigh and he was bleeding profusely. His face was starting to become pasty white and his breathing was labored.

Butch flipped open his Zippo lighter and lit the cigarette between his lips. He took in a deep breath and exhaled before coughing even harder.

"You know, Frank, I had you all wrong. All the years I heard what people said about you. That you were missing a few bolts and screws up top, but that wasn't the case, was it?"

Frank glanced at a smudge of blood on his face.

"You were probably the only one that knew this shit was coming. That's why I took your stuff. I thought, if anyone would have medical supplies that could get us through this, it would be you."

"Didn't you ever think to ask?"

"I did, you told me to get off your island or have you forgot?" He took another puff. "In reality you brought this upon yourself." He nodded and looked off towards the truck. "All this time you've been living by yourself, well, I hope you can live with yourself after what you've done."

Even though he was bleeding out, he wasn't the kind of man to go out that way. His right hand, which was out of view, came around in one fast smooth motion. Frank didn't even need to see the barrel before he unloaded four rounds into Butch's chest. His body convulsed for a second, and then relaxed.

Frank stood there for a few more seconds looking at his dead body before he crouched down and his eyes began to well up. Anxiety, fear, and panic made his body tremble. He wasn't given to killing. Nor did he find pleasure in taking a life. Instinctively he reached into his pocket for his meds but they weren't there.

Though he never fully knew Butch or those that had burned up inside the building, they were locals, folks who were a part of his daily life. He'd seen them working in the stores, out and about in town, and fishing by the river.

Crouched on the ground he couldn't believe it had come to this. He placed a heavy hand against his forehead and sat there for a few more minutes trying to catch his breath before rising and heading for the truck.

# Chapter 24

The bald one carrying the gasoline moved cautiously towards the house. He had a guy beside him eyeing the windows, and he was nervously moving his rifle around. Sal and Jameson were under the cover of trees, about fifty feet from them.

There was no discussion between the two; they knew what had to be done. As the men got closer to the house, the bald guy unscrewed the cap and began dousing the side of the house, moving along quickly, and at one point dropping the metal canister.

Jameson had crouched down into a position to take the shot. He was the better marksman of the two of them and he was certain he could take him out without any further threat.

Sal breathed heavily as he watched Jameson take the shot. The snap of the round echoed as the bullet struck the man in the side of his chest. He collapsed on the ground without being able to fully engulf the back of the house. There was a moment of exhilaration. A sense that they had accomplished what they had set out to do, but that was all smothered when they saw the flame in the other guy's hand, he tossed it and a burst of fiery red and orange followed as it caught the corner portion of the house alight.

As he turned to run, Jameson took him out.

Flames crept up the side of the house and two more men stepped out from the tree line and began unloading round after round in their direction.

Sal edged forward. "We need to get the kids out."

"I agree but wait a second."

Sal went to rush out into the clearing and towards the storm cellar when Jameson grabbed his leg and he collapsed on the ground.

"Are you an idiot? The moment you step into that clearing you are dead."

"I'm not letting them die."

Jameson clenched his jaw. "Go then, I'll cover you."

Sal raised his rifle and without any regard for aim he just began unloading rounds in the direction of the men while Jameson did the same. He sprinted across the clearing and landed hard on the cellar doors. Flustered, panicked, and wanting to throw up, he hurried to get the key in the lock. He'd just got it inside and twisted the lock off when a guy came around the side and fired at him. A bullet struck him in the shoulder and he collapsed. Fully expecting the guy to rush up and finish him off, he heard another crack and looked up to see Jameson rushing towards him.

"Go, go."

Using all the energy he could muster Sal hauled himself up and yanked open the cellar doors and literally dropped down into the basement. He landed hard, rolling over the concrete steps. He gasped in agony. There wasn't even time for Jameson to lock the doors, he launched himself inside and landed hard on top of Sal. Out of breath and gasping for air, he yanked up Sal and they rushed up the basement steps all the while hearing men coming from behind. As soon as they reached the top of the stairs they locked the door behind them and collapsed on the floor.

Gloria screamed as she saw Sal's bloody shirt.

"We need to get out of here, they've set the place on fire."

Zach was up on his feet though grimacing through gritted teeth.

"Ella, Hayley," he yelled. They were still firing rounds so Jameson went up to get them. Seconds later they emerged. Ella was shocked at the sight of another one of them injured.

"Listen up, we know two of them are dead, one is injured. That leaves three good men out there, that's all. They can't cover both exits."

"There's two on the north side," Ella said.

"The fire is on the south."

Already they could smell smoke as flames burst through one side of the house on the south corner.

"There's no easy way out of this. Okay. Here's what

we're gonna do," Jameson said. "I'm going to the north side and lay down some heat. Ella, you are going to have to fire from the south window, while the others make a break out the door."

They all looked at each other as though it was the last time they might see each other alive. It was like flipping a coin. Though in their case they had probably less chance of surviving. But if they didn't leave now they would die from smoke inhalation.

"Alright. Let's do this," Sal said rising to his feet. Coughing hard, Gloria had already brought the children down. They were huddled below a table with several items barricading off the sides.

"I'll go out first," Zach said.

"I'll be right there with you," Sal replied.

They moved into position.

"Ready?" Jameson yelled. The sound of Ella's gun erupting gave him his answer. He joined in firing rapidly in multiple directions. The gunfire seemed even louder as Sal flung the door open and one by one they rushed out.

He had his son Adrian beside him and was using his body to protect him. Gloria was doing the same with Bailey. Zach covered Jameson's daughter, Kiera. Though he didn't look to see if anyone was aiming a weapon at them, he figured he was inhaling his last breaths.

"Gabriel!" Ella shouted.

Sal turned his head to see several men rushing up the island and firing weapons at those who were attacking. Hope rose in his heart but only for a second. It was soon quelled as he turned to his right and saw Gloria hit the ground.

"Gloria!" he screamed.

He passed Adrian to Zach and he took him to the dense thicket while Sal rushed to Gloria's side. She was motionless, bleeding from the side of her face. Several gaping holes, one in the neck, another in the face. He rolled her lifeless body over to find his daughter had been struck as well. She was still alive but sucking in air rapidly and had this wild look in her eyes.

"Hang in there, baby," he said through the tears that

blurred his vision. He scooped her up and with pain in his shoulder he moved with purpose to get her to safety. He had no idea that Gabriel and the others had overtaken those attacking, all he saw was the face of his child staring back at him, trying to say something.

Collapsing to his knees he screamed for help but it was useless, within seconds Bailey took her last breath.

"No!" he yelled, rocking back and forth with her lifeless body.

* * *

Frank saw the fire from the boat as he made his way across the choppy waters. The smell of smoke reached his nostrils. His heart sank, not because the cottage that had been passed down from his parents was now gone, but because he had no idea if Ella and the others were still alive.

Fear drove him on as he opened the throttle and powered on to the island. As soon as he reached the dock, he powered down, killed the engine, and hopped out. He could hear yelling, and cries long before he had managed to make his way up the steep rocky incline.

"Ella!" he yelled. "Ella!"

His eyes scanned the people, some he recognized, others he didn't and then he saw her. Her face was blackened by smoke, but alive and unharmed. She rushed up to him and he wrapped his arms around her, holding her tightly as she wept.

Off to his left he saw Gloria, and then his eyes darted over to where the crying was coming from. Kneeling over his daughter's body, with Zach trying to console him, was Sal.

"No please. I didn't," a man said off to the right.

Another gunshot went off and it startled him. He turned to see Landon standing over a man. He'd shot him in the head. Days ago, perhaps he would have said something. Maybe he would have argued or taken offense to what had to be done but not now. Something had clicked inside of him. By the looks on the faces of everyone, the same had occurred in them. The need to feel safe took precedence over mercy.

Tongues of fire flickered high in the night sky, the heat warming their cheeks as Frank looked bleakly upon on what had been lost. And yet as he glanced at Ella's face, then at Sal's, he knew that buildings could be rebuilt, shelter could be found, but nothing could replace the loss of a family member.

Frank broke away from Ella and slowly made his way over to Sal while regarding the others who looked on with blank expressions. Frank placed a hand on Sal's shoulder and crouched down beside him. Sal turned, his cheeks wet and red with tears. No words were exchanged, only a hug.

When he rose to his feet, he cast his eyes over those that had come to help. Among them he saw Gabriel and Tyrell and the corner of his lip curled ever so slightly. Both gave a nod. He was pleased to see them alive, even if it had come at a heavy price.

"What now, Dad?" Ella asked taking his hand.

He didn't reply, instead he gazed at the fire as chunks of wood collapsed, and every crack and pop signaled years of memories evaporating into the air.

"We heal. Rebuild. And ensure this never happens again."

Frank cast a glance over his shoulder to Sal. He didn't know what dangers lay ahead, or what trials and tribulations they would have to endure, but he was convinced that whatever lurked beneath the surface, whatever might steal, kill, or destroy tomorrow, they would face it together.

* * *

THANK YOU FOR READING

Anxiety: (The Agora Virus Book 2)

Book 3 will be available in March 2017.

## A Plea

Thank you for reading Anxiety. If you enjoyed the book, I would really appreciate it if you would consider leaving a review. Without reviews, an author's books are virtually invisible on the retail sites. It also lets me know what you liked. You can leave a review by visiting the book's page. I would greatly appreciate it. It only takes a couple of seconds.

Thank you — **Jack Hunt**

# Newsletter

Thank you for buying Anxiety, published by Direct Response Publishing.

Click here to receive special offers, bonus content, and news about new Jack Hunt's books. Sign up for the newsletter. http://www.jackhuntbooks.com/signup/

## About the Author

Jack Hunt is the author of horror, sci-fi and post-apocalyptic novels. He currently has three books out in the Camp Zero series, five books out in the Renegades series, two books in the Agora Virus series, one out in the Armada series, a time travel book called Killing Time and another called Mavericks: Hunters Moon. Jack lives on the East coast of North America.

Made in United States
Orlando, FL
13 February 2023

29966248R00217